NO EASY REDEMPTION

by Sam L. Sullivan

ISBN: 978-0-9998226-6-1

Cover Design: Nathan Adam Sullivan
https://nathanadamsullivan.com

Dedicated to those for whom
redemption does not come easy

If we confess our sins, he who is faithful and
just will forgive us our sins and cleanse
us from all unrighteousness.
1 John 1:9
(New Revised Standard Version, 1989)

PROLOGUE

THE DAY had arrived. The day Jason had looked forward to. And dreaded. He wasn't ready. He would never be ready.

It was the third day of spring break. He was scheduled to work all day, but when he got the call, he left as soon as Cal could arrange to cover for him. Troy would have joked that Jason wasn't breaking the speed limit, just bending it a little. He tried to ignore the queasy feeling in his stomach as he made his way across town, frustrated by the traffic and the stop lights that conspired against him.

As the miles crept by and the minutes flew, he remembered how carefree his life used to be. He had planned to relish every minute of his final year of high school, his last chance to enjoy the carefree lifestyle of a teenager. But everything had changed the first week of July—July 4, to be exact. Ironic how a day called Independence Day had such a reverse effect on him.

CHAPTER 1

Tuesday, August 13, the previous year

Swinging his book bag up on his shoulder and dodging his way through the mass of humanity that made up the student body of Westfield High School, Jason didn't see the one face that meant the most to him.

"Oh, there you are!"

Jason turned to see Troy Kirkland weaving through the crowd. He'd known Troy since kindergarten. They'd been almost like brothers, although they looked nothing alike, Jason with his straight brown hair and brown eyes and Troy with his wavy red hair, gray eyes, and glasses.

"You seen Salena this morning?"

Troy smiled. Troy always smiled. It had started to get on Jason's nerves, since he had so little to smile about these days. "Good morning to you, too. But no. I haven't seen Salena. I thought the two of you broke up."

"Why'd you think that?"

"Haven't you heard the rumor?"

"What rumor?"

"Uh . . . the rumor that you and Salena broke up."

"Where'd you hear that?"

Troy shrugged. "Man, I don't know. I think it was from somebody who heard it from his neighbor's cousin on his mother's side."

Jason's brow wrinkled. "I have to find Salena. Come on." He motioned for Troy to follow, and the two of them made their way to the top of the bleachers, where they could scan the crowd below.

"There she is." Troy pointed toward the other side of the gym.

The bell sounded for everyone to be quiet. Speaking into a microphone, Mr. Petry began his annual spiel: "Welcome back. Hope you had a good summer. It's time to get down to business. Do your best." *Blah-blah-blah.* He ended by instructing the juniors and sophomores to leave the gym.

After the underclassmen shuffled away, the 60-plus seniors were instructed to scrunch into a small section of the bleachers so Mr. Petry and Ms. Carter, the 12th grade counselor, could give them a brief outline of their senior year and tell them how to finalize their class schedules. The things Jason had looked forward to now lacked appeal.

As he and Troy took their seats, Jason again searched the crowd for Salena. She wasn't there.

* * * * *

ON THE first day of school, students ran through an abbreviated version of their new schedules and left at noon so the faculty could meet after lunch to compare enrollment numbers and iron out problems they'd encountered.

Cal had asked him to come in and work the afternoon and evening shift. Jason didn't mind. He was glad to have the job. The café wasn't a bad place to work, and Jason liked earning his own money. It not only gave him some independence but also seemed to make his father happy. Not that he cared much about that. He and his dad hadn't seen eye to eye on anything in years.

When he got home from work that evening, he tried to phone Salena. As usual, he got no answer. It had been almost three weeks since she'd answered his calls.

Unlike Tuesday, the rest of the week was whole days. He kept an eye out for Salena. They had no classes together, but they still walked the same hallways and ate in the same cafeteria. Surely their paths would cross now and then. So why didn't he see her?

Jason had always liked school and usually made good grades in all of his classes, even math, his least favorite. His favorite classes were band and choir. He'd made first-chair clarinet and had tenor solos in almost every choir concert the past two years. It didn't endear him to the jocks, not even his brother Derek, who graduated last year and enlisted in the Army.

But Jason didn't need approval from those guys. He just hoped they would leave him alone, which they mostly did.

That was an unusual thing about his relationship with Salena. It didn't matter that he wasn't a sports nut, even though she was a star volleyball player and expected to receive a full athletic scholarship at the local university, Arkansas State.

Jason counted on a music scholarship. If Dad had to pay for college, he'd insist Jason choose something more traditional—meaning more lucrative.

Unlike Salena, Jason planned to go somewhere across the state. He hadn't decided which school yet. It partly depended on who offered him the scholarship. The farther away, the better. He didn't put it quite that way to his parents.

* * * * *

Friday, August 16

"HEY, JASON!" Troy almost collided with Jason as he spun around the corner by the cafeteria. "I just saw Salena. She's headed toward the gym."

He knew he'd get into trouble for running in the hall, but with only a minute before the tardy bell, he had to take the chance. Only one teacher noticed him, and she was new this year and didn't know his name. "Hey, stop running in the hall," she shouted as he sped past. He felt a little guilty for pretending not to hear.

He rounded the corner just in time to see Salena at the water fountain outside the gym.

"Hey, girl." He paused to get his breath. "Where you been? I been looking for you all week. How come you don't answer my calls?"

Salena's brown eyes only glanced into Jason's. "Look, we can't talk right now. We'll be tardy."

"What'm I supposed to do? It's like you've been avoiding me on purpose."

Salena stared at the floor for a couple of seconds, as if counting the green and white tiles. "I haven't been here every day." When she looked up again, her eyes still seemed to be avoiding his.

The silence was broken by the bell. Salena started to say something else but was interrupted by a shrill whistle from the gym.

"Hey, García," yelled the girls volleyball coach. "You heard that bell. Get in here."

Salena started for the door, and Jason grabbed her arm. "Wait! I have to know what's going on."

With a scowl on his face, Coach Miller stepped into the hall. "Okay, Sadler, I don't know what's your problem, but you need to get to class."

Jason hung on to Salena's arm another second.

"Call me tomorrow," she said as she freed herself from his grasp.

"Yeah, like that'll do me a lot of good."

"I'll answer this time. We need to talk."

What did she mean by that? he wondered as Salena rounded the corner. That's what he'd been trying to do for weeks—talk. He hadn't been the one preventing it. Surely Troy wasn't right about the breakup. Jason knew *he* hadn't said anything to start such a rumor. Was it only a rumor?

CHAPTER 2

Saturday, August 17

WHEN HE phoned Salena, she answered, as she had promised, and they arranged for him to come to her house around one. He went ahead and dressed for work. He would have to drive the opposite direction to get to Salena's house, which meant about thirty extra minutes of driving time. And who knew how long the "talk" would take?

One good thing Jason could say about his dad, he had helped him buy his first car. Dad agreed to pay up to $5,000 for a "good used car." The catch—with Dad, there was always a catch—was that Jason had to figure out a way to pay for tags, insurance, gas, and maintenance. This forced Jason to get the job. Chalk up another victory for Dad.

But at least he had a car, a black 2004 Kia Spectra with just north of 100,000 miles. It wasn't exactly the sleek cool-mobile he had always dreamed of for his first car, but—he almost smiled when he thought of this—Salena didn't seem to care what kind of car it was. It had four wheels and started every time he needed it to. Until today.

A few minutes past noon, he turned the key, but nothing happened. He tried again. And again. And again.

"You gotta be kidding me!" He pounded the steering wheel with both fists. "Why today of all days?" No one answered.

His mother wasn't at home, so he had to ask his father to drive him to work. Of course, he couldn't ask Dad to take him to Salena's house. When he called to tell her he wasn't coming, he apologized profusely and hoped she believed he was telling the truth. She seemed to take it pretty well.

"See you Monday?" he asked just before ending the call.

He couldn't help but notice she didn't reply right away. "Um . . . I don't know. Maybe." And then she was gone.

* * * * *

HE FELT like he was being punished. He would be stuck at home all weekend, so when Dad picked him up after work, Jason called Troy and asked him to come over. Luckily, Troy's dad's car was available.

"You heard anything else?" Jason asked as they hung out in his room Saturday evening.

"About what?" Troy flashed that annoying grin.

Jason heaved a loud sigh and drummed his fingers impatiently on the top of his desk. He knew Troy knew exactly *about what.*

"I haven't heard any more rumors, if that's what you mean." Then Troy said something that almost caused Jason to blow through the ceiling. "But I don't know why you keep chasing after that girl anyway. Can't you see she's done with you?"

"I can't believe you would say that. You're supposed to be my friend."

"I *am* your friend, dude. Who else is gonna tell you the hard truth?"

"She's just going through something, that's all. But how can I help her if she won't even tell me what it is?"

"All the more reason to give it up. Who needs that kind of grief?"

Jason gazed at the floor. "To be honest, not long ago I did think about giving up. It seemed like Salena and I were drifting apart. That was before July Fourth. Everything's different now. It changed my life, you know?"

"So I've noticed. I still can't believe you got yourself into such a thing."

It wasn't supposed to happen. His parents had been gone, and Jason and Salena were alone in the house only a couple of hours. It was long enough.

He knew he wasn't perfect, and he knew everyone made mistakes, but he couldn't forgive himself. Even so, he thought he and Salena should be closer now. Apparently, she didn't feel that way. She had hardly spoken to him since then.

"You and me both," said Jason. "Unfortunately, it was easier than you might think."

CHAPTER 3

Monday, August 19

"YOU GET the dung beetle fixed?"

"The what?"

"Oh, come on, you know that's what your car looks like."

He had to admit Troy was right. That's when Jason named his car D.B. No one had to know what the letters stood for. He knew Troy wouldn't tell.

"Yeah, I had to buy a new battery at Walmart yesterday. Set me back eighty bucks. My dad loaned me the last ten. I hate owing him money, but it's better than having to ride in the same car with him."

They were sitting in the bleachers, where the students always gathered before school. Jason searched the crowd for Salena. Some of the volleyball girls were clustered at the top on the opposite side of the gym, but Salena wasn't among them. He decided to go over and ask about her.

"No, we ain't seen her," said one of the girls. "She's been missing a lot of school lately."

"That's not like her. Why has she been absent?"

"You need to ask *her*."

"I would if she'd let me."

One of the other girls spoke up. "I don't think she likes you following her around all the time."

"I don't follow her around."

The girls all made weird faces at one another.

"I'm just trying to talk to her. What's wrong with that?"

"Ain't nothing wrong with it," said the first girl, "except for one thing. She don't wanna talk to you."

"She wanted to talk to me Saturday. I had car trouble and didn't make it."

"Whatever," the girl said, and they all turned back to their own business.

* * * * *

AT LUNCH, Jason happened to be at the right place at the right time and spied Salena as she entered the cafeteria. He ran over and stopped her.

"Hey, Salena. Can we have lunch together so we can talk?"

"I'm not eating today. I'm just looking for someone."

"Obviously not me."

She glanced across the room toward the table where the volleyball girls were sitting. Jason noticed all of them were watching Salena.

"Let's go somewhere else," he said. Salena didn't move. "Come on. Please!"

She stepped back into the hallway and sat down on a bench across from the principal's office. Jason hoped Mr. Petry didn't see them. He tended to go ballistic when errant students managed to escape their designated confines.

Jason felt a definite chill as he perched on the bench a couple of feet from Salena, close enough they could talk without being overheard.

Salena was the first to speak. "Okay, it's time you knew. You're not going to like what I have to tell you. I don't like it either."

"Babe, what is it? You're killing me!"

Salena took a deep breath and pushed a strand of dark hair from her face. Then she stopped and put her hand over her mouth. Without a word, she jumped up and ran away. Jason glanced across the hall—the warden wasn't in sight—and ran after her.

He turned a corner just in time to see her dart into a restroom. Determined not to let her get away so quickly, he waited. Soon she returned, looking a little pale.

As he stood there still breathing heavily from his sprint down the hallway, Salena said, "Jason, I'm going to have a baby."

CHAPTER 4

"A BABY!" said Troy Monday afternoon. They were in the band room, waiting for marching practice. Only a few students had arrived so far, and no one was close enough to eavesdrop. "What did you say when she told you?"

"I couldn't say anything. We ran out of time."

"No wonder she's being so weird. What are you gonna do?"

"I don't know yet."

"I know what I'd do. I'd gas the dung beetle up and head for Canada."

Jason flinched and his eyebrows furrowed.

"You're right," said Troy. "Too cold. Maybe Mexico then."

"This isn't a joke."

"I know. I'm just glad it's not me. Not that it ever could be, considering my luck with girls."

There was an awkward silence as some of the other band members filed in.

Troy leaned in and spoke quietly. "You know I have to ask. Are you sure it's your kid? Hey, don't give me that look. I just mean, are you sure no other guy has been . . . you know . . . with Salena?"

"You say that again, I'll smash that snare drum over your head."

Troy smiled and pushed his glasses up on his nose. "I'll take that as a yes. Is she gonna keep it?"

Jason's head jerked up. "That hadn't even crossed my mind. I don't think she has a choice. She's Catholic."

"She gonna quit sports?"

"I hadn't thought about that either. You ask too many questions, you know it?"

"Hey, dude, somebody's gonna ask them."

"Yeah, I know."

"When will you see her again? I mean, now maybe the two of you can quit playing cat-and-mouse, since obviously the cat is out of the bag. Or the kitten is *in* the bag, you might say."

"I'm supposed to go over to her house this Saturday. She wants me there when she tells her grandparents."

"They don't know yet? Oh, man! Her grandpa's gonna kill you."

"I hope not. Or maybe I should say I hope so."

* * * * *

Saturday, August 24

D.B. STARTED this time, and Jason found Salena in the backyard, sitting in the swing the two of them used to play on a few years ago. Her twelve-year-old brother Benny was kicking a deflated soccer ball across the grass.

"Jason!" Benny shouted. "Where you been? I been missing you."

"Hey, B," Jason said as Benny ran over. They bumped fists and then did a wiggly exploding motion with their fingers. Jason had taught Benny the greeting the first time they met. Benny's family had been impressed. He'd never interacted with strangers, but he took to Jason like he'd known him forever. "Oh, I been around. You staying out of trouble?"

"Yeah." He glanced over at Salena. "No."

"He's doing better," Salena said from the swing as Benny went back to kicking the ball.

"Hey, you." Jason offered Salena his hand. "You ready to do this?"

She stood up. "Not really. I've been dreading it ever since I found out."

"You know you could have told me sooner. You didn't have to keep it to yourself."

"I didn't know what to do. And I didn't know how you'd take it."

Jason held both of Salena's hands as they stood facing one another. Now that he knew what was going on, he couldn't help noticing Salena looked a little plumper than she used to, especially in her middle. It didn't spoil her looks, though. At least not yet.

"Salena, listen. I want you to know I'm sorry. I know we made a big mistake. I promise it won't happen again. Is that why you've been avoiding me?"

"Partly. But I know it won't happen again. I won't let it."

"You don't have to do this alone. I'm here."

Salena's dark eyes filled with tears.

"Did you hear me? I'm willing to take full responsibility."

"Yeah, I heard you."

"Your folks here?"

"Mommi's in the kitchen. I think Poppi's in the garage. Hey, Benny, we're going inside for a while. Stay in the yard, you hear?"

Benny gave the floppy ball another kick. "Okay."

Jason and Salena found Arianny García sliding a sheet of chocolate chip cookies from the oven. Her gray hair was tied in a tight bun at the back of her neck, and she was wearing a wrinkled white house dress covered by a stained yellow apron.

"*Buenos días, Señora García.*" Jason had taken two years of Spanish and enjoyed practicing with Salena's family.

"*Hola*, Jason. I don't see you in a long time."

"Yes, ma'am, I know." He glanced at Salena. "I've been kind of busy."

"Mommi, can Jason and I talk to you and Poppi a minute?"

"*Sí*. I'll call him." Mrs. García made a motion indicating they should sit at the table. "I'm making *galletas*, Jason. You like one?"

"They smell great, but no, *gracias*."

When Sergio García joined them, he was wearing a sweat-soaked white T-shirt and dirty blue sweatpants with ragged sneakers. He obviously had not shaved in a few days. His thin gray hair was covered by a camouflage cap, which he hung on the back of his chair. As he plopped heavily at the table, Jason noticed a faint odor of gasoline mingling with the fragrance of Mrs. García's cookies.

"*Bienvenido, mi amigo*," Mr. García said, slapping Jason on the shoulder.

"*Buenos días, Señor García*. How's the roofing business?"

"It is good. We are busy all the time."

Salena took a deep breath. "Poppi. Mommi. Jason and I have to tell you something."

Mr. and Mrs. García glanced at one another, and Mrs. Garcia reached for her husband's hand.

Salena swallowed hard and forced herself to speak. "I'm going to have a baby."

Mr. García's jaw dropped as he took a deep breath. Mrs. García sat with her hands folded in her lap.

"Mommi, you knew?"

"We live in the same house. You are like my own *hija*. How could I not know?"

Jason recognized the Spanish word for daughter.

Mr. García frowned at his wife. "And you don't tell me?"

"I knew Salena would tell us when she was ready."

Mr. García scowled at Salena. "Just like your *mamá*."

Salena fought back a sob. "No, Poppi, I would never do drugs and all those things that ruined her life."

Poppi's scowl shifted to Jason. "So. What are your intentions?"

"We haven't had a chance to discuss it. Salena didn't tell *me* until yesterday."

"I'm not going to keep it," said Salena.

"By this you mean what?" asked Mommi.

"I found an abortion clinic in Little Rock."

"Oh, Salena, no!" Mrs. García covered her mouth with the hem of her apron.

"It's the only way I can make things like they were."

"Things will never be the way they were." Tears threatened to tumble from Poppi's eyes. "You should have considered the consequences before you went too far."

"You must bear the child, and you must be married," said Mommi.

"No, Ari. We are talking about our own family this time. They are too young to be married. I will not give my consent. I do not want this irresponsible boy to be part of my family."

"Poppi, you've always liked Jason."

"That was before he did this to you. Before I knew he is no better than your father."

"Please stop comparing Jason and me to *Mamá* and *Papá*. Jason is not like *Papá*."

Jason looked down at his hands, which lay limply in his lap.

"Every child has a right to live and have both mother and father," said Mommi.

"I don't want to be married." Salena's voice was almost pleading. "And I don't want a baby."

Jason's stomach twisted. He hated to admit that he didn't want it either. He hung his head, a pang of regret rising in his throat.

"I'm afraid, Mommi," said Salena. "Do you think God wants me to bring a baby into the world if I can't take care of it?"

"God had nothing to do with it." Poppi thrust a dirty fingernail in Jason's direction. "You and *this boy* did it on your own."

Jason's stomach lurched again at Poppi's words.

Poppi swiped his hand across his wet cheek. "You were to be the first in the family to finish high school. It would make us so proud if you went to college. How is it going to happen now?"

"Sergio, we knew Salena would have a family someday."

"Of course, Ari. I knew it would happen *someday*. But not now. And not with *this* boy!"

A third time Jason felt as if he had been punched in the stomach. Salena sat with her head down, teardrops plopping into her lap.

"I will take you to talk to Father McNair."

"No, Poppi. I won't go."

"Yes you will!" Poppi's brown eyes flashed. "I am not asking. I am telling."

Salena glanced at Jason. His heart ached for her. "I'll go with you if you want me to," he said.

Salena seemed about to say yes, but Poppi cut her off. "No! You have done enough. If Father McNair needs to talk with you I will let you know. I think we have seen enough of you for a while." Without so much as a glance in Jason's direction, Poppi stood and stormed back to the garage.

In the tense silence Poppi left behind, Salena, Jason, and Mrs. García stared at one another. Finally, Mrs. García spoke. "I agree with your *abuelo*. You must talk to Father McNair."

"I haven't told my parents yet," Jason said.

"You must tell them."

"Yes, ma'am, I know."

When Jason and Salena went back outside, they found Benny sitting in the swing, staring at the ground. The floppy soccer ball lay forgotten in a corner of the yard.

"Hey, B, what's wrong?"

"I was just thinking about something."

"Yeah? Like what?"

"Like, what the janitor said when he jumped out of the closet?"

"What did he say?"

"SUPPLIES!" Benny began to laugh.

"You got me there, B." Jason gave Benny another fist bump, followed by the wiggly hand motion.

"Later, guys." Jason headed to his car. "I'm going to talk to my parents now. Wish me luck."

CHAPTER 5

Sunday, August 25

JASON'S PARENTS weren't home when he returned from Salena's house on Saturday, so he didn't get to talk to them until Sunday dinner. He knew it wasn't a good time, but he might not have another opportunity.

The family ate in silence, only briefly mentioning the morning's church service or requesting more bread or potatoes. After they finished dessert, Jason asked his parents to stay at the table. This was unusual, and he could tell by the look on their faces they were worried.

"Dad, I want to repay the ten dollars you loaned me for the car battery." He took the money out of his shirt pocket and laid it on the table.

"Thanks. I wasn't worried about the money. Is that all that's bothering you?"

"No. I have to tell you something."

"Oh no." His mother grabbed her napkin as if she needed something to hold onto. "You're not in trouble at school, are you?"

"Of course not. Or at least not as far as I know."

"What have you done?" asked Dad. "Did you wreck your car?"

"No. Can you just listen to me for a minute?" Both of his parents stared at him. "I got Salena pregnant."

His mother's mouth fell open, and she covered it with her hand. "Oh Jason, why on earth?"

"How long have the two of you been having sex?" Dad asked.

"We haven't."

Dad raised his eyebrows and cleared his throat.

"I mean . . . just one time. We didn't intend to go so far. We've hardly even spoken since then. I only found out a few days ago."

"Are you sure it's yours?"

"Don!"

"Well, we have to know, Susan. Our son's not about to pay for some other kid's mistake."

"I'm sure," said Jason.

"And how do you know she didn't plan this?"

"What?"

"I know that girl's background. Who would blame her for doing anything she can to escape it?"

"Don!" Mom repeated more forcefully this time with a twist of the napkin.

"Salena's not that kind of girl, Dad."

"And you know this how?"

"I've known Salena forever. She wouldn't do something like that. I know you never liked her, but she's a good person. It wasn't her fault. It just happened. We both wish it hadn't."

"Well, that train's left the station, hasn't it?" Dad leaned back in his chair and crossed his arms. "Your brother never did anything like this."

It was true. Derek made all the right decisions. He was a star athlete and now a soldier. Jason was so different from his father and brother, he sometimes wondered if he'd been adopted.

"Unfortunately, I'm not Derek. I know he's your favorite."

"Jason! Don't say that."

"It's true, Mom, and you know it. I'm sure Derek will come back and fall right into Dad's footsteps. D. & D. Sadler, Certified Public Accountants. Perfect!"

Dad responded with a grunting sound.

"I'm just the stupid little brother."

"I never said you're stupid, Jason."

"You don't have to say it."

"I just wish you had a better focus in life."

"And there it is. I'll never be able to please you." The silence weighed heavily on Jason's slumped shoulders. He hesitated a moment and then flung back his chair and stood up. As he swayed on his feet, unsure whether to say more, Mom got up and began clearing dishes from the table. She was crying. Jason hated to see his mother cry, especially if he caused it.

He went up to his room and got his phone to call Salena. She didn't even say hello.

"How'd it go?"

Jason glanced toward the door. "Hold on, I never have any privacy." Salena waited while he went outside. In the driveway, he rolled down all of D.B.'s windows and slid into the driver's seat.

"It didn't go so well. Mom cried and Dad's ready to disown me. Neither of which surprised me, by the way."

"At least they didn't put you out of the house . . . did they?"

"Not yet." Jason puffed out a long breath. "How have your folks taken the news? Are you in solitary confinement?"

"Actually, no. I managed to convince Mommi and Poppi I'm going to be more careful the rest of my life. After all, what's the worst that can happen now?"

"Speaking of which, you're not serious about having an abortion, are you?" The silence on the other end of the line made Jason's stomach hurt. "Salena, please! Don't I get a say in this? After all, I'm the one who got you into it."

"It so happens, Poppi and I talked to Father McNair today, too."

"Yikes! And how did *that* go?"

"Well, if it makes you feel better, I'm no longer sure it's a good idea to end my pregnancy."

"I know how the Catholic church feels about abortion."

"Not to mention my grandparents."

"I hope they don't send you to a nunnery or something," Jason said in an attempt to lighten the mood.

"Hmm. Now there's a frightening thought. I've never heard of a pregnant nun."

Jason glanced toward the back of the house to make sure no one was eavesdropping. He got out of the hot car and leaned against a shaded part of the hood. "I'm sorry your last year of high school has started off so rough. How are you keeping up? I mean, missing so much school and all."

"Mr. Petry and Ms. Carter are helping me."

"They know?"

"I spoke to Ms. Carter before school started. She helped me put together a plan before we talked to Mr. Petry."

"Petry? You mean he has a heart?"

"Who knew, right? Actually, he's been very understanding. He and Ms. Carter promised they wouldn't pass any of this information to anyone. Of course, I won't be able to hide it forever. I don't know what Petry told my teachers, but they've been helping me, too."

"It's good we've both told our folks."

"That doesn't mean it's going to be any easier."

"Yeah, I know."

"Hey, look, Jason, I gotta go."

"Sure. See you tomorrow?" Another infuriating pause. "Salena?"

"Still here."

"See you tomorrow?"

"Probably."

"Prob—?" The phone went silent. Jason pounded his fist on D.B.'s hood. His whole world was spinning out of control because of Salena, and all she could say was *probably!*

CHAPTER 6

Monday, September 2

SCHOOL WAS out on Labor Day. With the universe and his boss conspiring against him, as always, Jason had to work most of the day. His shift didn't begin until eleven, but he couldn't see himself sitting at home until then. In fact, he'd rather be just about anywhere else. He called Troy and arranged to meet him at the mall, which was just down the street from Cal's Café.

He didn't have to drive past the church building, but for some reason, he did. He was surprised to see Brother Marsh's car parked outside. His mother would have said it was providential the preacher was at the church building today. Jason wasn't sure he believed in providence, but he did believe in coincidence.

Something unexpected had happened on Sunday. The sermon topic was forgiveness. Jason had heard it all before, but he'd never thought much about it until now. He had considered talking to Brother Marsh afterward, but it didn't work out. Besides, his parents would have butted in.

As soon as Jason pulled into the church parking lot, Brother Marsh came out and headed toward his own car. Jason took this as a sign it wasn't the day to talk to the preacher after all. Relieved, he spun D.B. around and headed back out. Seeing Jason there, Brother Marsh threw up his hand in greeting and walked over and motioned for Jason to roll down the window. He was wearing jeans and a blue polo shirt. Jason didn't remember ever seeing the preacher dressed so casually.

"Hello, Jason. What brings you to church on a day that's neither Sunday nor Wednesday?"

"Hi, Brother Marsh. I came to talk to you, but if this is a bad time . . ."

"Oh, no, not at all." He looked at his wristwatch. "Matter of fact, I have a little time on my hands. Let's go inside where it's cooler."

Jason checked the time on his phone. He had about an hour before work.

Jason had been in Brother Marsh's office a few times before. It was small and cluttered with books and papers, but it was comfortable. It smelled like coffee and peppermint. Maybe peppermint coffee. Brother Marsh walked around his desk and sat down, motioning for Jason to sit in one of the chairs on the other side of the desk. "Dee and I were talking about you just the other day."

Daveon Watson and his wife Evy were two of the few black members of the church. As the church's youth minister, Dee had managed to fit in quite well. The teens didn't care what color his skin was.

"Me?"

Brother Marsh nodded. "He told me how involved you've been in the youth group and what a positive role model you are for the younger guys."

Jason looked down. "I appreciate Dee's vote of confidence, but it's actually been a while since I was able to participate in any of the activities."

"So, how can I help you?"

Jason swallowed hard and studied the top of the desk as he cleared his throat. He didn't know whether Brother Marsh knew about his predicament, and now that they were face to face, he was embarrassed to talk about it. He looked down at his hands and then said the first thing that came to mind. "I paid attention to your lesson on forgiveness yesterday."

Brother Marsh chuckled. "You say that like it's unusual for you to pay attention to my sermons."

"Most of the time I feel like you're preaching to someone else."

"Yeah, unfortunately that's what *everyone* seems to think. But not this time?"

Jason shook his head. Brother Marsh waited. Jason appreciated it, but it also scared him a little. "You said everyone needs forgiveness sometimes."

"Um-hm."

Jason started to speak again, but the words caught in his throat. To his horror, his eyes began filling with tears.

Brother Marsh stopped smiling. "Including teenage guys who seem to have it all together." He leaned forward and crossed his arms on the desk in front of him. "What's on your mind, son? Maybe you'll feel better if you talk about it."

And then the story spilled out. After about five minutes, Jason was both relieved and appalled he'd said so much. "That's why your sermon hit me so hard."

"Because you're the one who needs forgiveness this time."

Jason looked down and nodded silently.

"From whom?"

Jason raised his head. "My parents. Salena. Her grandparents."

"And?"

"God." He had never thought he would say that. "I know I need His forgiveness."

"Forgiveness from God is no more than a sincere prayer away. I can help you with that if you like."

"No, thanks. I can do it on my own."

"Anyone else?"

"The baby. What kind of life will it have? It has no choice."

"That's an insightful and mature thing to say."

Jason sat with his head down for a moment. "The worst part is that I don't think I'll ever be able to forgive *myself*."

"So you think you're more important than God?"

Jason raised his head. "No, sir. I would never think that."

"If He thinks you're worth redeeming, why would you question Him?"

"I don't deserve redemption."

"That's a terrible way to feel. I know. I've been there."

"You? I thought preachers led perfect lives."

Brother Marsh smiled. "Now, wouldn't that be nice! Truth is, when I said everyone needs forgiveness, I was including myself."

"So, what am I supposed to do? How can I make it right?"

"Good question. Of course, it's different for everyone. The real question is, what are *you* going to do?"

"I don't know yet. Salena has considered abortion. Her grandparents are against it, of course. They're Catholic."

"Well, that's one thing I agree with them on. Murder is murder, no matter whether the victim has been born."

"You think we should get married?"

"That presents the next question. How do you feel about Salena?"

"You mean do I love her?"

"Well, yes, but considering your age—seventeen? Eighteen?

"We're both seventeen."

"To be honest, I have a hard time believing the two of you really know that kind of love."

"I like her. I like her a lot. And I miss her when she's not around. But love? I don't really know. That doesn't change the fact that we've created another human being. It seems selfish to base our choices solely on our feelings for each another."

"Did you happen to be paying attention a couple of weeks ago when I preached on being unequally yoked?"

Jason had to confess he didn't recall that sermon.

"Second Corinthians 6:14 instructs us not to be unequally yoked with unbelievers."

"You think Catholics are unbelievers?"

"No, but they don't believe some things the way we do."

"Haven't such marriages happened?"

"Sure. And some couples make it work pretty well. But it brings its own set of problems, particularly for families like yours who are strong in their own beliefs."

"I'm not sure I'm that strong."

"Have you talked to your mom and dad?"

"Yes, sir. Dad's ready to disown me."

Brother Marsh chuckled. "Oh, I don't think you need to worry about that. I happen to know your dad loves you very much."

"He has weird ways of showing it." Jason glanced at the time on his cell phone. "I have to be at work at eleven." He stood up. "Thanks, Brother Marsh. I feel better. A little anyway."

"Don't forget that prayer for God's forgiveness."

"I won't."

"I hope you'll work on the forgiveness you owe yourself, too?"

"I'm afraid that'll be a little harder. I've gotten myself into a situation I'll never get out of, and other people's lives are messed up because of it."

"You still need to try. Why not let God help you with that?"

"Yes, sir, I'll try." Jason shook Brother Marsh's hand. "Thanks again."

"Any time, Jason. Always glad to help. Let me know how this turns out, huh?"

"I will." Jason started for the door.

"Oh, and one more thing. A few minutes ago, I commended you for your work with the youth group. I wonder what kind of influence you'll have on the younger guys now."

"You think I should quit the youth group?"

"Oh, no. Just be careful what you say and do. I won't share this with anyone, of course. But everyone's going to know sooner or later."

"Yes, sir. I understand."

Just as Jason reached the car, his phone rang. It was Troy. "Hey, dude, where are you? I'm sitting outside the mall."

"I forgot."

"You forgot? I'm worried about you, man."

"Thanks. I'll call you after work, okay?"

"Yeah, whatever. Not holding my breath."

CHAPTER 7

HE MANAGED to function somewhere close to normal
for a few weeks. His dad was as hard to get along with
as ever, and he figured Dad felt the same way about
him. Mom seemed to have accepted the situation. In
her work as a public health nurse, she had seen all
kinds of situations. She sometimes asked about Salena
and acknowledged it was probably harder for her since
she hadn't planned to get pregnant and was so young.

Salena stopped missing so much school. Though
their paths seldom crossed, Jason made a point to
search her out before school and at lunch. Once in a
while she condescended to sit with him, but most of the
time she preferred to sit with her friends. He didn't like
it but figured she needed some girl time—not that those
girls had any idea what she was going through. He

wondered what they said about him but thought it was probably better he didn't know.

* * * * *

Thursday, September 19

TODAY WASN'T to be one of those routine days. Before the first bell rang, Jason, Salena, and Troy had just gotten settled in the bleachers when Carl Moore, one of the smart-aleck jocks, walked by below and saw them together.

"Hey, look guys," Carl said to his cronies. "There's Lover Boy with his *chiquita*."

Troy was the first to respond. "Get lost, C-Moore," he yelled.

"Don't call me that, Nerdwad."

"Ignore him," said Salena. "I don't care what that creep says."

"I do," said Jason.

"Eh? What'd you say baby-daddy? You're taking your *chiquita* out for a walk? Did you hold her hand? Oh yeah, I forgot, you're *way* past that."

Jason clenched and unclenched his fists. "Shut up, Carl," he shouted down the bleachers. Everyone sitting nearby turned and looked up at him.

Carl looked at his friends. "He did *not* tell me to shut up. Did anybody else hear him tell me to shut up?"

"Why, I believe I did," said one of the boys.

"You gonna let him get away with it?" said another.

"Better believe I'm not." Carl turned and shouted up to Jason, "Maybe you'd like to come down here and tell me to shut up. You think your little *chiquita* can spare your lovin' for a minute?"

Though he knew he'd get killed, Jason stood up and started down the rows of bleachers. He didn't intend to pounce on Carl, but when he reached the bottom, his momentum sent him tumbling off the bottom step. Everyone scattered as the two of them collided, and several people started chanting, "Fight! Fight!"

Without thinking, Jason pulled back his fist to punch Carl in the face, but someone caught his arm. He turned to see Troy pulling him backward.

"Let go, Troy!"

"Yeah, let go of the boy, Troy," said Carl. "I need a clear shot of his pretty face."

There was a loud whistle, and Coach Miller appeared. "Hey, you guys, break it up." He stepped between Jason and Carl. "You two come with me."

The next thing Jason knew, he and Carl were walking side by side as the three of them headed for Mr. Petry's office. Carl glanced over at Jason and sneered. At that instant, with his insides churning like a tornado, Jason hated Carl more than he'd hated anyone in his life.

Mr. Petry was out, so the coach instructed them to sit on separate benches just outside the door.

"I'll get you for this," Carl said with another sneer.

"Hey, I didn't start it. I was minding my own business and you came along with your big talk."

"Well, all I can say is, you better be glad Coach showed up. I'd a busted your face."

"Not without a fight, you wouldn't."

When Mr. Petry arrived, he called the two boys into his office and sat them down. As each told his own story, Mr. Petry wrote everything in an Incident Report. "I'm calling your parents. You're both suspended three days."

Jason's mother got the call at work, and she arrived about thirty minutes later. Her face didn't give away how she felt, but Jason knew he'd hear plenty later. She instructed him to get his car from the student parking lot and go straight home.

When they got home, Jason went to his room. Nothing much would be said until his dad got home. Then he would be grounded the rest of his life.

* * * * *

IT WASN'T quite the rest of his life, but it seemed almost as bad—a whole month. Dad was concerned how this looked for the family and what people would say about his parenting skills. Of course, he had to remind Jason that Derek never got into fights at school. Jason knew it was because everyone liked Derek, not to mention that his jock reputation kept even the biggest goons from challenging him.

After Jason thought everything had been said, Dad's next remark hit where it hurt most. "It's that girl. You never had any trouble until you started messing around with her."

"Salena had nothing to do with it."

"According to your mother, Mr. Petry said you were fighting over her."

"We weren't fighting over her. Carl insulted her. Was I supposed to just sit there and let him?"

"If you had, you wouldn't be suspended."

"It wasn't Salena's fault."

"Well, I want you to stay away from her."

"No, Dad. That's not fair!"

Jason's mother came to his defense. "Don, whether we like it or not, Salena is carrying Jason's baby. He can't just forget about her, which a lot of boys would have done."

Dad's face reddened, and his jaw clenched and unclenched, like he was biting hard on the words before he spit them out. "Well, what do *you* propose we do? Just turn them loose to make more illegitimate babies?"

"Dad, I promise that won't happen. Believe me, this is not the direction I would have chosen for my life right now. But it is what it is. What kind of man would I be if I didn't step up?"

Mr. Sadler gazed at his son for a moment, then he looked at his wife, let out a long breath, and turned back to Jason. "Okay, the two of you seem to have this all figured out." He threw up both hands. "I'm out of it. Let's see how well *you* handle it." Before he stomped out the door, he paused and looked back. "But you're still grounded for a month. You will drive only to school and work. When you come home, you will hand your phone over to your mother."

"And what about Salena?"

"I think you should give it a rest while you're grounded. No phone calls, no spending time with her at school unless it's absolutely necessary."

"Don!"

"Don't *Don* me, Susan. Give me that much say-so, will you? I only want what's best for our son."

"At least let me tell her." Jason almost cringed at sound of his own pleading voice. "She has to know what's going on."

Mr. Sadler looked at his wife and then at Jason. He didn't say anything else, which Jason took as agreement.

Jason went immediately to his room. When he dialed Salena's number, she answered quickly. She seemed to take the news well. In fact—was it his imagination?—she almost sounded happy about it.

CHAPTER 8

With his days full of classes, homework, choir and band practice, half-time marching shows at football games, and work, Jason hardly realized he was grounded, except for having to surrender his phone when he got home. He had to admit he was glad to have some time to think about everything, including his relationship with Salena.

At first, he thought about her a lot. But some days he didn't think about her at all. When he caught a glimpse of her at school, she never seemed to be looking for him, and he eventually realized he didn't look for her so much either.

When he did see her, he couldn't keep from noticing how much bigger she was getting. He usually had no problem putting the whole thing out of his mind, but he supposed her changing body constantly reminded her of him, not in a pleasant way.

Through the rumor mill, he learned Salena had dropped out of volleyball and would lose the scholarship she counted on. And worse, she might not even finish high school. All the more reason for her to be angry with him.

But was *he* any better off? Salena's life wasn't the only one disrupted. He wasn't the one having the baby, but his life would never be the same either. What right did he have to go across the state and leave Salena to deal with the baby alone? Everything he had wanted and worked for had been snatched away, all because of one mistake, admittedly a big one.

In the beginning, Salena had talked about ending the pregnancy. Could this be the best option after all? Had he been stupid to object? As soon as he thought of this, he felt another pang of guilt. Even if the baby wasn't conceived in love, which should have been the case, it had as much right to live as Jason did. Just as important, it did not deserve his resentment.

It? The thought suddenly struck him that just as the baby deserved to live, it also deserved to be considered a person instead of *it*. Boys tended to run in the Sadler family, so until he learned differently, he would think of the baby as a boy. His son. The thought scared him a little. No, it scared him a lot.

* * * * *

Friday, October 18

JASON ARRIVED at school early and took his place at the top of the bleachers where he could spot Salena when she arrived. Troy hadn't shown up yet, so Jason had no trouble keeping his eye on the door.

Exactly ten minutes before the first bell rang, Salena and her friends swarmed through the wide doors. She walked in the middle of the others as if they were her bodyguards. He hurried down and got her attention.

"Hey, Salena, can I talk to you a minute?"

She sighed and shifted her eyes to the bodyguards. They seemed to take this as a signal to split. She and Jason moved to a corner of the gym where there weren't many students.

"I'm proud to say, as of yesterday I am officially ungrounded," said Jason.

"Good for you."

"I've missed you."

"Really." This was more a statement than a question.

"Yes, really."

Salena gave a slight shrug. "What do you need to talk about?"

"I want to spend some time with you tomorrow night. You know, to celebrate my ungrounding."

He wasn't just disappointed when she didn't respond right away. The feeling seemed awfully close to anger. He forced himself to wait for an answer.

"Okay. Pick me up at six."

* * * * *

Saturday, October 19

HE GOT off work at five and hurried home to shower off the smell of fried food and change clothes. He pulled up at Salena's house at 5:50.

Mr. García was using a blower to clean autumn leaves off the driveway. Before an awkward conversation could begin, Salena appeared. She was wearing stretchy pants with a loose shirt to accommodate the second trimester of pregnancy.

With a stern glance at Jason, Mr. García instructed Salena to be home no later than ten. Ten o'clock seemed like an early curfew on a Saturday night, but Jason needed to stay on Poppi's good side. "Yes sir," he said as he helped Salena into D.B.'s front seat.

"What do you want to do?" he asked Salena as they pulled away. "Catch a movie? Grab a burger? No, wait, I'd probably just fall asleep in a dark theater and I've smelled enough burgers for one day."

Salena almost smiled. "Thanks for letting me decide."

"Anyway, can you even eat burgers? I mean . . ." He pointed at Salena's bulging mid-section.

Salena grinned. "I'm sure the baby likes burgers as much as I do. But maybe we're in the mood for pizza. That is, if I'm allowed to make a suggestion."

"Pizza it is." Jason steered the car toward Vinnie's, their favorite pizza joint.

After they placed their order at the counter, Jason led Salena to a quiet booth in a corner and sat opposite her so they could talk. He was the first to break the silence. "So, what's the latest? No more morning sickness, I presume."

"No, thank goodness. I've had a couple of checkups. All's well so far."

"That's good. Is everything okay with your *abuelos*?"

"As far as I can tell. They seem to have accepted it. Not that they have much choice. It will be hard on them with a baby in the house. They already have their hands full with Benny."

"Does he still give them a lot of trouble?"

"Not as much as he used to."

"Poor guy. Do you think your grandparents would mind if I come over and say hey sometime?"

"I think they'd be okay with it. They know how much Benny likes you."

"He's a good kid. It's tough what he's been through. Speaking of which, do you ever hear from your dad?"

"No. Benny doesn't even remember our father. I wish I didn't."

"Do you know where he is?"

Salena shook her head. "Not exactly. I told you *Papá* is in prison, didn't I?"

"You don't tell me *anything* anymore. What did he do?"

"Not sure. Poppi thinks I don't need to know all that stuff."

"And what about your mom?"

"Mommi talks to her once in a while. Poppi doesn't want Benny and me to have anything to do with her either."

The pizza arrived and they ate in silence. As the minutes ticked by, Jason was tormented by what wasn't said, the weighty topics that had to be discussed. When the pizza was almost gone, he took the chance to bring up the subject that had been bothering him.

"Have you decided what you're going to do?"

"I haven't told you that either?"

"Last I heard, you hadn't made up your mind."

"I'm keeping the baby. I mean . . . at least I'm going to *have* it. I may have to drop out of school. I'm not sure about anything past that."

"Your grandparents will help, won't they?"

"They'll do what they can. I hate that I've caused such a burden for them."

"Not just you, don't forget."

"Oh, I haven't forgotten. I intend to hold you eternally responsible." She said this in a joking manner, but Jason knew many a truth is said in jest.

"I plan to help, you know."

"Oh, yeah? How you gonna do that when you go away to college?"

"I'm not going away. I've decided to stay here and go to ASU."

"Really?"

Jason nodded. "I might start part time. Or maybe I'll wait a year or two. That way I can get a job that pays better."

"That's nice. I probably won't go to college."

"Sure you will. It'll just take us both a little longer than we planned." After a short pause, Jason dropped a bombshell. "Let's get married."

CHAPTER 9

SALENA'S HEAD jerked up, and her mouth fell open.

"Marry me," Jason said.

"Jason, I—"

"Look, it's the only way we're going to make this right. It isn't going away. We got ourselves into it. No one else should have to pay the price. You said yourself your grandparents deserve better. So does the baby. *Our* baby."

"Jason, we're seventeen. Don't you think we're a little young to be married?"

"We're too young to be parents, too, but here we are."

"Anyway, Poppi already said he wouldn't give his permission, remember? And you think your parents would consent?"

"I got the idea your grandparents actually believe we should be married. How hard would it be to change Poppi's mind? And I don't care what my parents think. I'll figure out a way to convince them."

Salena's face softened. She slid her hand across the table and covered Jason's. "Look, I appreciate your efforts to make this right. I really do. But I—"

"You don't have to answer right away. Take some time to think about it. I'd say take all the time you need, but we don't have that luxury." He slid his hand from under Salena's and covered both of her hands with his. "Think about it, okay? How about Thanksgiving break? That should be long enough."

Salena didn't answer.

"*Okay?*"

"Okay," she said at last.

* * * * *

Monday, October 21

"You WHAT?" Troy shouted when Jason told him the news at school.

"I asked Salena to marry me."

"What were you thinking?"

"I'm not sure what I was thinking. But I have to do *something*, don't I?"

"What did your mom and dad say? Have you told them?"

Jason nodded. "Yesterday afternoon. Typical response. Dad hit the ceiling. Mom cried. They'll get used to the idea eventually. Salena's supposed to give me her answer at Thanksgiving."

"That's a month away. You want to wait that long?"

"Not really, but I will if I have to. I know she'll say yes."

"What makes you think so?"

"She has to."

"Dude, I hate to be the one to break it to you. No, she doesn't."

"But she will."

"And what if she doesn't?"

"I'll deal with that if I have to. But she will."

"By the way, does your brother know about any of this?"

"Not sure how much Mom and Dad have told him. I haven't spoken to Derek since he left home."

"What? That's sick!"

"What difference does it make to *you*?"

"Man, I'd give anything to have a brother like that. Wait, who am I kidding? I don't want to be his brother. I want to be *him*."

"Trust me, no you don't."

"Who wouldn't? Have you *seen* that guy?"

"I shared a room with him until I was twelve. Mom used to put us in the bathtub together. I've seen all I want to see."

Troy scrunched his face. "Gross!"

"Just when we were little."

"Still, too much information, man!"

"You're the one who brought it up."

* * * * *

EVEN THOUGH Jason wasn't grounded this time, he felt it best to leave Salena alone. He made a point to speak to her when she gave him the chance, but he was careful not to make her feel pressured. He still got nervous around her entourage, as he didn't know how much they knew. Actually, it seemed like they ignored him as much as ever—maybe more.

One good thing happened during those weeks. Jason decided to work on improving himself. He stopped relying on his mother to wake him up in the morning and began setting an alarm thirty minutes early so he would have time to go into his brother's room and work out with his weights. After several days of sore muscles, he began to feel like he was making some progress. He noticed a little added bulk across his shoulders, and—was it just wishful thinking?—he seemed a little less flabby around the middle. He wasn't sure what he was trying to prove or whom he wanted to impress, but he was starting to feel better about himself.

* * * * *

Monday, November 25

SOMETHING TOTALLY unexpected happened on the first day of Thanksgiving break. Salena's grandfather called early that morning and asked Jason to come to their house. Benny was missing.

Hurrying across town, Jason felt bad for neglecting Benny. He had offered to go check in with him but never found the time. Also, his need to give Salena her space would have made a visit to her house seem like an imposition.

It was a chilly day, and as he parked in front of the house, Jason was surprised to see so many people gathered in the yard. There were two police cars. Salena told him the police had said they normally wouldn't have responded so quickly. It wasn't unusual for a kid to be missing for a few hours. But due to Benny's special needs, everyone felt a heightened sense of urgency.

Mr. and Mrs. García looked relieved when they saw Jason. Mr. García said Benny had been wondering why Jason never came to visit. This morning after breakfast, Benny disappeared from the backyard. It was at that point Mrs. García recalled Benny saying something about going to look for Jason. She hadn't considered he actually would.

Mrs. García said Benny was wearing faded jeans and a red jacket. Jason and Salena hopped into D.B. and started cruising the area, checking behind bushes and buildings and in ditches and culverts. When they came to a place where shrubbery blocked their view, they got out and called Benny's name.

Around noon, additional police were called in, and an announcement was aired on television and radio. Jason was scheduled to go to work at two. At one thirty, he phoned the café and said he wouldn't be at work today. Cal said he understood. He'd seen the reports on television.

Later in the afternoon, Jason drove by an open area about five miles from Salena's house. In the distance, he happened to see a flash of something red. He and Salena got out of the car and started across the field.

"Benny!" they called repeatedly.

There was no response, but at one point, Jason heard something moving in the tall grass. He called again. "Hey, B, what's going on? Come on out, *mi amigo*."

Then he had an idea. "Hey, B, what did the janitor say when he jumped out of the closet?"

Silence.

"Remember, B? Remember what you told me? What did the janitor say when he jumped out of the closet?"

"SUPPLIES!" came a shout from the tall grass.

Jason turned in that direction. "That's it! That's a good one. You got any more?"

There was a pause, and then the voice asked, "What did the farmer say when he couldn't find his tractor?"

"I don't know. What *did* the farmer say when he couldn't find his tractor?"

"He said, 'Where's my tractor?'"

Jason and Salena both laughed. "That's another good one, B."

And then Jason spied Benny hunkered down behind a bush.

"There you are," Benny said. "I've been looking all over for you."

"Well, looks like you found me. You ready to come home?"

"No!" Benny shouted. "There's something I have to do first."

"What's that?"

As Jason walked closer, Benny reached out and the two of them bumped fists and made the wiggly hand motion. Then Benny headed for the car. "Let's go. I'm hungry!"

Salena's grandparents were elated when Salena called and told them they'd found Benny. When the three of them got back to the house, Jason was surprised to see his father standing in the yard with Salena's grandparents. Dad had never seemed interested in getting acquainted with Mr. and Mrs. García.

As soon as they got out of the car, Mrs. García rushed over and hugged Benny. Mr. García did the same and then scolded Benny for running away.

"I didn't run away. I was looking for Jason. I wanted to find out why he doesn't like me anymore."

"I still like you, B. I just don't get to come around much." He looked at Mr. and Mrs. García and then at Salena.

"Well, this has to change," said Mr. García. "You are welcome here any time. That is, if it is okay with your father."

Mr. Sadler shrugged. "I think I'd be fighting a losing battle if I said it wasn't."

Jason exchanged a smile with Salena.

Ari García hugged Jason like he was her own long-lost son. "Thank you for helping us find Benito."

"No problem. Benny's my bud. I don't want anything to happen to him."

After the police, family, and neighbors dispersed, Jason and Salena sat in D.B. with the motor and heater running. Jason checked the gas gauge. The red hand was uncomfortably close to "E."

"I have an answer for you," said Salena.

"Answer? To what?"

"Aren't you the guy who asked me to marry him a couple of weeks ago?"

"As a matter of fact, I do believe it was me. I didn't expect to talk about it today."

"Good a time as any."

"So you've decided?"

"I think you're right. We should get married."

"Really? You sure?"

"As a matter of fact, no. I'm not sure of anything these days. Well, there's *one* thing I'm pretty sure of.

After the way you helped with Benny today, I don't think I'm going to find a better person to marry."

"Not to mention that you're carrying my baby. That's gotta count for something."

"That, too."

Jason glanced around the house and yard. Convinced no one was watching, he leaned over and kissed Salena. To his surprise, she actually seemed to kiss him back.

* * * * *

Wednesday, November 27

THE NIGHT before Thanksgiving, the church held a special service. Afterward, Jason happened to run into Daveon Watson.

"Hey, Jase. Haven't seen you around much lately."

"I know, Dee. I been sorta busy. A lot on my mind."

"So I hear. Been missing you in the youth group."

"I thought I might not be welcome anymore." He glanced across the room, where the preacher was chatting with some other people.

"Brother Marsh?"

"He's afraid I'll be a negative influence."

"Well, I don't know what he said to you, but I'm sure he didn't mean you're not welcome."

"Even though I messed up big time?"

"Of course. True, we don't want any of the other kids to follow that particular example, but you're still one of mine, you know. I mean, I'm the official youth minister and you're still an official, uh, youth."

Jason looked down at the floor.

"You know you're not the first person in the world to make a mistake."

"Yeah, I know. But it's the first time for me. I mean . . . one this big."

"Mind if I tell you a little secret?"

"I guess not."

Dee gazed across the room again, where his wife Eveanna was laughing with some of the girls. Then he glanced from side to side and spoke quietly. "But for the grace of God, I could have been in your shoes."

"You?"

"Evy and I dated less than a year, and we knew from the start we were going to get married. But intending to be married and even being engaged is not the same

as being married. More than once it would have been awfully easy to cross that line. Her daddy caught on and put his foot down. Said if I ever took advantage of his daughter, I'd pay for it. I didn't know how he intended to accomplish that, but I got the picture. We'd planned to be married the following spring, but we decided to make it a December wedding."

"I appreciate you telling me this. I feel a little better knowing I'm not the only stupid person in the world."

Dee laughed. "Believe me, brother, if there ever was an award for *stupid*, you and I are a long way from being the first to qualify."

"How old were you and Evy when you got married?"

"I was twenty, she was nineteen."

"Salena and I are both seventeen."

"I know. Truth is, the odds are stacked against you. I'm sure you realize that."

"Yeah, everyone keeps telling me. But that doesn't mean we can't make it work."

"True. Good luck. Let me know if I can help."

"Thanks, Dee." Jason headed for the door.

"Hey, Jase, how about giving us some help tomorrow."

"At the shelter?"

Dee nodded. "Almost all the kids are going to be there. We could always use one more."

"Sure. See you around noon?"

"Actually, we'll start setting up about ten thirty."

"Fine. See you then."

CHAPTER 10

Thursday, November 28

THANKSGIVING WAS one of the few days of the year when Cal's Café was closed. Jason's mother had been happy when she thought at least one of her sons would be present for dinner, but she and her husband both said they were proud of Jason for giving his time to help at the shelter.

The temperature outside was near freezing, but the dining room was warm and filled with tantalizing aromas when Jason arrived about eleven, just as preparations were beginning in earnest. The ladies of the church, together with adult volunteers at the shelter, had baked turkeys, hams, cornbread dressing, mashed potatoes, green beans, rolls, and every kind of dessert imaginable.

Extra tables and chairs had been set up, and some of the teens were bustling around spreading orange and yellow plastic table cloths, topped with small decorations.

Just before noon, the guests started arriving. Most of them were strangers. Jason was assigned "mashed potato duty." As he plopped spoonful after spoonful of potatoes on Styrofoam plates, he greeted everyone with a smile.

When some of the first pans were almost empty, Jason noticed a young man coming through the line. He looked to be in his mid-twenties, had shaggy blonde hair, and was wearing ragged jeans and a stained gray hoodie that said, "What's the difference between a puppy and a liberal? The puppy stops whining when it grows up."

"Like the shirt," Jason said as the man passed his station.

"Thanks," the man replied. "Guess you're not a liberal."

"Definitely not."

"Me neither."

"Happy Thanksgiving," Jason said as the man moved on to the green beans.

"You, too."

A few minutes later, Jason was surprised to see the young man coming back through the line with another plate. Seeing Jason's expression, the man smiled. "This ain't all for me." He pointed toward a table where a young woman and two little girls were seated. That's when Jason noticed the man was wearing a wedding ring.

"It's okay." Jason hurried to the front of the line and grabbed another empty plate. When he got back to his own station, he said, "Here. Why don't you fill up two at a time? Save you some trouble."

"Thanks," the man said as Jason piled a double portion of mashed potatoes on both plates.

Jason watched as the man reached the end of the line again and rejoined his family. The mother was wearing baggy sweat pants and a loose shirt that hung mid-thigh. The little girls wore what appeared to be pajamas, and the smaller girl coughed now and then. Both parents kept wiping the kids' noses but seemed to be fighting a losing battle as they also stuffed food into the little mouths.

Jason's first impulse was to feel sorry for the young family. He wondered what circumstances had caused them to be at a shelter on Thanksgiving. Both parents looked healthy enough to work, but they obviously couldn't afford daycare, so the mother had a good reason to stay at home.

What's the dad's excuse? Jason wondered. What kind of father doesn't provide for his children? But at least this father was still here, unlike Salena's dad. Jason suddenly felt a rare appreciation for his own parents. He knew his mom didn't make much money. She'd often mentioned she worked more for the satisfaction of helping others. For all Dad's faults, he'd never failed to provide well for his family.

"Hey!" said a voice at his right side. "Hey, Jason! You're holding up the line."

"Oh, sorry," he said to the girl who was dipping green beans. He resumed spooning potatoes but kept an eye on the young family. After they dumped their empty plates, the mother and the bigger girl put on jackets that seemed too thin for such a cold day. The girl's jacket looked about two sizes too small. It probably would have fit the smaller girl, but Jason soon understood why the bigger girl was wearing it. The dad slipped on his ragged corduroy coat and stuffed the smaller pajama-clad girl into the front of it before tugging the zipper up, leaving just enough of an opening for the child to breath. Watching through the front door, Jason saw the family cross the street and disappear down the sidewalk.

Before he left, Jason made a point to look for Dee and found him and Eveanna sweeping the kitchen floor.

"Jase, thanks for helping out today."

"No problem. Hey, do you or Evy know that young couple that was here? The ones with the two little girls?"

"Mm, not really," said Dee. But we can check and see if they signed in. It wasn't required, but some of them did."

Evy checked the sheet. "This is probably them. Lynn and Stephanie Smith."

"Any idea where they live? I saw them walking down the street toward the government housing."

"Yeah, that's probably where. Aside from the few who are staying here at the shelter, I figure most of our guests came from there."

Dee emptied the dustpan into a nearby trash bag. "Why do you ask?"

"Just wondering."

CHAPTER 11

Friday, November 29

WHEN JASON proposed to Salena—was it actually a proposal, or more like a suggestion?—he'd believed marriage was the best option. Now he wasn't so sure.

His emotions had been all over the place the past few months, and yesterday's experience at the shelter had changed his outlook. Again. He wondered where all those people were today, especially the young family he had seen. Was the father out looking for a job or just sitting around waiting for the next handout?

Jason imagined himself as that young father gathering free food for his family and wiping snotty little noses. Could he put himself and Salena in such a hopeless situation?

And what about the baby, the *person* he'd helped create? How many times had he been reminded, and even said himself, that the baby didn't ask to be conceived? Didn't it—*he*—deserve better?

Jason made up his mind. He would not put all of them in that situation.

After work that afternoon, he called Salena and asked if he could come and talk to her. She said okay. When he arrived at her house, Salena's grandmother greeted him with a smile and invited him inside. Mr. García was out on a roofing job. From his room down the hallway, Benny heard the voices and popped out.

"Hi, Jason!" he said as the two of them did their fist-bump routine.

"Hey, B-man. Got a joke for me?"

"Not right now."

"Check you later, okay?"

Benny disappeared back down the hallway.

Mrs. García started to sit down but then stopped. "I should leave the two of you alone maybe?"

"No, ma'am. I think you should hear what I have to say."

Mommi and Salena sat on the couch across from Jason.

Jason took a deep breath to steady his nerves. "Salena, have you told your *abuela* what we talked about the other day?"

"If you mean about getting married, *sí*, she told me," said Mrs. Garcia. "Sergio and I are not sure how it will turn out. The two of you are so young. But it is only right Salena be married before the baby is born. It will not wait. See how big my *nieta* is getting?"

"That's what I came to talk about." Jason's eyes bounced between Salena and her grandmother. In spite of his dread, he knew he had to say the words he came to say. "Salena, I don't think we should get married."

Salena's mouth fell open. "What? It was your idea."

"I know. Something happened that changed my mind."

Salena sat back and crossed her arms as tears began to spill from her eyes.

"What about the baby?" said Mrs. García. "It will be *ilegítimo*. Think of the, how you say, stigma."

"I believe things have changed. I don't think there's as much stigma as there used to be. At least not here."

"You will leave Salena to raise the child alone? Sergio and I are not able to care for a child at our age."

"I intend to help as much as I can," Jason said, although he knew it wasn't much to offer.

There was fire in Salena's eyes as she stood and went to the front door. "Get out!"

"Let me explain."

"You needn't bother."

"Salena, listen! What kind of future will we have if we get married now? I'm not abandoning you. I'm just thinking of everyone's best interest."

"Especially your own."

"Also yours. And the baby's. What kind of life can we give it?"

"What choice do *I* have?"

"What about adoption?"

"You want me to give my baby away?"

"Not too long ago, you wanted to *kill* it." As soon as he said these words, he wished he hadn't.

Salena's hand shook as she covered her mouth and sobbed openly.

"I'm sorry, Salena. Really! I shouldn't have said that. But adoption's the only way the baby will have a good life." He looked at Mrs. García, who was now also in tears. Without another word, she left the room.

"You think my family isn't good enough to raise *your* baby?" Salena spat out the word "your" like it tasted bad.

"No, that's not what I meant. I—"

Salena stood with the door open. "I said get out!" she screamed.

"Salena, please listen!"

"You *are* like my *papá*! You only care about yourself. I hate you!"

"Surely you don't mean that."

"How do you know what I mean? I don't even know you anymore."

"Well, maybe it's because you always hide from me."

Salena paused for an instant, as if Jason's words had struck a chord. Then she lashed out again. "I'm sorry I talked Poppi into giving his consent. I wouldn't marry you if you were the last man on earth. I hate you! I never want to see you again."

"What about our baby?"

"It's not *our* baby. It's *my* baby. I can manage on my own. I don't need your help." With tears streaming down her face, Salena stood in the doorway.

As Jason slid past her, Benny's voice called out from his bedroom. "Hey, Jason. Knock knock."

Jason glanced at Salena and stopped. In spite of how he felt about Salena at the moment, he didn't want to let Benny down again. "Who's there?"

"Boo."

"Boo who?"

"Hey, why are you crying?"

Jason left. He *was* crying, but he hoped Benny didn't know.

CHAPTER 12

"I CAN think of one good thing about this situation," Troy said when Jason told him the news that evening.

"Oh, really. And what would that be?"

Troy flashed that obnoxious grin. "This is all happening to you, not me."

"Thanks for the sympathy."

"She actually said she hates you?"

"Yes, actually. Twice."

"Man, that's tough." Troy extended both arms and took a step toward Jason.

Jason stepped back. "Dude, you are *not* gonna hug me."

Troy grinned sheepishly. "Oh, sorry. I couldn't help myself. You're just so needy."

"I'm not needy."

"What? Man, you're the local poster child."

"Well, I'm not *that* needy."

"I just calls 'em as I sees 'em. You know what they say, there's none so needy as the poor soul who doesn't know how needy he is."

"No one says that."

"I just did. Remember, I love you, man."

"Troy, never say that again."

"Man, you sure know how to hurt a guy. Anyway, look. Who's been telling you to drop that girl? I knew a long time ago you were headed for trouble? I think I'm, like, psychic or something."

"More like psy*cho*."

Troy raised one eyebrow and gazed toward the ceiling, giving a slight nod. "I'm willing to accept that possibility."

* * * * *

THE WEEKS between Thanksgiving and Christmas were a blur. The band and choir practiced every day during class and sometimes after school for the Christmas concert. Jason was given a clarinet solo in "Sleigh Ride" and a tenor solo with the choir. The director asked him to sing "Mary's Little Boy Child." How appropriate, he thought. Sometime around the end of November, he had learned through the grapevine that Salena had found out the baby was indeed a boy.

Naturally, she hadn't shared this information with him. The two of them never spoke. In fact, he had hardly seen her since the day after Thanksgiving, when he delivered the awful news. When he passed her in the hallway or happened to see her in the cafeteria, she didn't even look his way. The same couldn't be said for her bodyguards. At least one of them managed to give him *a look* at every opportunity.

* * * * *

Sunday, December 1

IN SPITE of the unseasonably warm weather, Jason's mother was inspired to start decorating the house early for Christmas. When they were kids, Derek and Jason had always helped their mom and dad decorate the tree. This time, Mom seemed resigned to doing it all by herself. She'd somehow coerced her husband to haul the big artificial tree down from the attic and was in the process of single-handedly lugging all the boxes to the living room. Feeling sorry for her, Jason volunteered to help, since he didn't have to work Sunday afternoon.

It would have gone faster if Mom hadn't stopped every few minutes to examine the collection of old homemade ornaments. Some of them hadn't been out of the boxes in years, but Mom felt compelled to drag them out this time. She spent the most time staring at the brittle paper and foil decorations, the ribbon-wrapped Styrofoam balls, and the hand-written Christmas cards Derek and Jason had made when they were in elementary school. Jason noticed that she sniffed and wiped her nose a few times as she hung the objects in prominent places on the tree and leaned the old cards up on the mantle among this year's greenery and tinsel.

* * * * *

Tuesday, December 3

JASON SMILED when he looked out the window Tuesday morning. Apparently, Mom had a direct line to the

Lord, for the temperature had dropped sharply the past couple of days and the ground was dusted with snow. The snow continued on and off the rest of the week, but the roads were never icy enough to cause school to be cancelled.

The December 14 Christmas concert went off without a hitch. Jason's clarinet solo was marred by one sour note, but his tenor solo went perfectly. Several people commented on the feeling he seemed to put into the song. He didn't tell anyone, but his inspiration came from his thoughts of a different little boy child. Not Mary's.

In his *spare* time, Jason managed to keep up his workout routine. He was definitely building some muscle and had recently noticed he could comfortably cinch his belt up another notch. He knew he'd never be another Mr. Universe like his brother, but he had to admit he was proud of himself. He didn't know how proud he could be until a week later, when Carl Moore gave him the chance to find out.

CHAPTER 13

Friday, December 20

THE LAST week of the semester was crammed with exams. School let out early on Friday, and Jason offered to drive Troy home before going to work. As they headed down the steps in front of the school, Troy hummed "Here Comes Santa Claus" under his breath.

"You're in a holiday mood," Jason said, hoisting his bookbag onto his shoulder.

"Two weeks with no school! Are you kidding me?"

"Must be nice for a lazy bum such as yourself."

"Yup!" Troy began to sing aloud as they headed to the car. "Bells are clangin', children sangin'."

Jason glanced over. "I like your version better than the original."

"You mean that's not how it goes? How about this? Lights are blinkin', children stinkin', the mall is smelly and bright."

They reached the parking lot just in time for Troy's song to be interrupted by some guys talking nearby. Jason recognized one of the voices.

"I heard she dropped him like a rock. Apparently, the choirboy was good for just one thing. Besides singing, that is."

"Better look out, Carl," said one of the toadies. "There he goes right now. You don't want to make the choirboy angry, do you?"

"Ohhh, nooo! I wouldn't want to do that."

As he turned and glared at Carl, Jason's nostrils flared and his jaw tensed the way he'd seen his dad's do when he was angry.

Troy tapped him on the shoulder. "Forget it, man. Let's just go."

"Yeah," said Carl. "Better listen to your boy Troy before you get whupped."

Jason's pulse raced as his fists clenched and unclenched around the strap over his shoulder.

"Uh-oh," said one of the other toadies. "Looks like Choirboy's getting mad again."

"Am I right, Choirboy?" said Carl. "Did the little Mexican chiquita need you for just one thing? I hear that kind of girl needs to start having babies early so they can get on welfare and get free food and stuff."

Months of pent-up rage exploded to the surface. Without a word, Jason let the bag slip off his shoulder. Before it even hit the ground, Jason was pounding Carl with both fists, hardly aware Carl was punching back.

By that time, a few other kids had gathered around. Most of them just stood and watched, but eventually a couple of hefty guys stepped in and managed to pull Jason and Carl apart.

"Here comes the coach," said one of the guys. "You don't want him to catch you, you better get out of here."

Jason scrambled to his feet, leaving Carl writhing on the ground. He felt something trickling down his chin. Swiping it with the back of his hand, he discovered his lip was bleeding. With a rush of satisfaction, he noticed that so was Carl's. A stream of blood also gushed from Carl's nose. He looked dazed, like he didn't know what had hit him.

"From now on, you need to leave me alone," Jason said as one of Carl's guys helped him to his feet.

"Okay, okay," said Carl. "I don't need no more trouble. My old man'll kill me if I get suspended again."

"And never insult Salena again. Understand?"

"Yeah, yeah. Ain't gonna be no problem." Carl and his crew headed toward his truck.

"Everything okay here?" Coach Miller had arrived on the scene as the spectators scattered.

"Sure, Coach, we're good," said Jason.

"What happened to your face?"

"Oh, me and Carl just needed to settle a few differences. Right, C-Moore?"

Carl stopped and looked back. One hand covered his bloody nose and lip, but his eyebrows were scrunched together in a scowl. "I guess so."

The coach glanced from one boy to the other. "So you're good now?"

"*I* am." Jason extended his hand. "C-Moore?"

"Yeah, sure," Carl said with a quick handshake, not even looking back.

Coach Miller eyed the two boys for a moment and then glanced at his watch. "Well, you guys have a merry Christmas. That includes you, Kirkwood."

"*Land*," said Troy. "My name's Kirk*land*."

"Whatever." The coach headed for his own car.

"Thanks, Coach," said Jason.

Coach Miller looked back. "For what?"

"Oh, uh, nothing. Merry Christmas to you, too."

CHAPTER 14

His Friday shift began at two o'clock. After he worked his scheduled four hours, Jason asked if he could stay longer. Cal looked relieved, saying one of the other employees had asked to go home early.

"I'll work all day tomorrow, too."

"What's with you? You ain't become one of them work-a-holics like your old man, have you?"

"I don't think there's much danger of that. Just need a little extra money."

Cal smiled. "'Tis the season, huh?"

"Yes, sir."

"Gettin' something special for your girl?"

"Um . . ."

"Never mind. Not my business. By the way, what happened to you? You get in a fight?"

"Um . . ."

"Again, not my business. Long as it don't keep you from showing up on time."

"Sure, Boss, no problem."

* * * * *

Saturday, December 21

JASON MANAGED to avoid his parents Friday evening and Saturday morning. He doubted his dad would pay much attention, but he could count on his mother to question him about the fat lip.

Saturday was a cold, windy day, and a hint of snow was in the air again. When he got to work at eleven, the café was swamped with shoppers who'd rushed in between mad dashes for those last-minute Christmas items. Most everyone was in a holiday mood. After his day's work, Jason counted fifty-four dollars and seventy-five cents in his apron pocket. Added to this week's paycheck, it should be more than enough.

He glanced at the clock on the wall. It was almost 7:30. He knew stores would be open late. He clocked out and ran and hopped in D.B.

At the store, it took him only a few minutes to make his purchase.

* * * * *

Monday, December 23

JASON FELT like a stalker as he sat in front of the government apartments a couple of blocks from the homeless shelter. Actually, that was exactly what he was doing, stalking someone. His busted lip still hurt a little bit as he smiled at the thought.

It was another overcast day. The air was cold and damp, as if the forecasted snow could start any minute. The gas gauge showed about half full, but he couldn't afford to be wasteful. He switched off the motor, bundled his jacket closer around him, and tugged his knit hat down over his ears. He hoped he wouldn't have to wait long as he kept his eyes on the row of apartments. A few of the residents had strung small strands of lights across the roofs of their porches, and about halfway down the street, a curtain was open, framing a small Christmas tree inside.

He got lucky. After about fifteen minutes, just as light snow began to fall, he saw someone scurrying along the sidewalk on the other side of the street. He recognized the tattered corduroy jacket of the young father he had met at the Thanksgiving dinner.

As the man passed, Jason pretended to be looking for something in the glove box of his car. It not only made him less easy to recognize but blocked the man's view of the passenger seat, where Jason had stashed a shiny green sack containing two boxes. He resumed spying as the man passed and became visible in the side mirror. The man took a key out of his pocket and opened the door to Apartment 105, next door to the one with the Christmas tree.

As soon as the door shut, Jason grabbed the green sack and ran through the blowing flurries toward the apartment. After dropping the sack on the porch, he punched the doorbell and ran back to his car. He drove down the street but stopped close enough to see the door of the apartment in the rearview mirror.

The young man stepped out and immediately noticed the sack. Soon, his wife appeared, followed by the two little girls. The girls grabbed the colorful sack and ripped the boxes open out on the porch. Each girl held a pink coat with matching hat and mittens. Jason congratulated himself on choosing the sizes. He was certain the coats would fit a year or two.

The young man stepped to the edge of the porch and looked up and down the street.

"Merry Christmas," Jason said as he hit the gas and sped away. Nobody heard, but he didn't care.

CHAPTER 15

Wednesday, December 25

JASON USED to like Christmas. When he and Derek were little, their parents went all out. The boys usually got everything they wanted, although Jason never asked for much. This year, he didn't ask for anything. It seemed too selfish.

Mom's big thing was clothes. She seemed to think no teenage boy could have too many socks or too much underwear. And woe be unto any mother who would allow her child to wear either with holes in them. It didn't matter no one else would know. *She* would know.

Dad's gifts were also practical—a Walmart gas card, a card for a free oil change, and new floor mats to replace the ones Jason was certain had come with D.B. way back in 2004. As mundane and predictable as his parents' gifts were, Jason appreciated them more since he had to start paying for those things himself.

Things were different this year. Even with all the lights twinkling on the tree and the gas logs blazing in the fireplace, no one looked happy. Mom seemed to be dabbing her eyes every time Jason looked at her. He presumed it was mostly due to Derek's absence. When he didn't make it for Thanksgiving, they were sure he would be home for Christmas.

Jason gazed across the room at the chair by the fireplace where Derek always sat when the family exchanged gifts on Christmas morning. As much as he hated to admit it, he, too, missed his big brother. This was the first Christmas the four of them hadn't been together. But it might not be the last. Derek had recently informed the family there was a chance he would be deployed to Afghanistan sometime next year.

He knew his parents' melancholy mood was also somehow mixed up with his own situation. "My children grew up much too fast," he'd heard his mother say on more than one occasion. He wondered if she would be happy again when she had grandchildren to spoil at Christmas. But he was in no hurry to find out. Not just yet.

* * * * *

HIS BOSS Cal hadn't been wrong when he'd guessed Jason needed money to buy Salena a gift. The truth was, Jason had delayed shopping because he had no idea what to buy. None of the usual things seemed appropriate. Last year, he'd given her a promise ring. It had gone over pretty well, though neither of them knew exactly what he was promising. All of that was now "wadded under the bridge," as Troy would say.

And what about the baby? Should Jason buy him a gift? Salena's little boy child wasn't due until April, but that didn't mean he didn't deserve *something*. An unsettling ache crept into Jason's chest when he realized this might be the only chance he would ever have to give his baby son a Christmas gift.

But he wouldn't go shopping today. Even though some of the stores would be open later, he thought he should hang around the house on Christmas Day. It seemed like the right thing to do for his mother's sake.

He was pretty sure it didn't make any difference to his dad.

* * * * *

Thursday, December 26

AFTER SPENDING some time on Derek's weights and taking a quick shower, Jason called Troy. He would pick him up around ten o'clock, and the two of them would go shopping for the gifts Jason had been wondering about.

"Man, I don't know nothin' about shopping for girls and babies," Troy said as he slid into D.B.'s passenger seat.

"Me neither. Guess it's time to learn."

The first store they came to was Target, just down the street from Troy's house. It was full of people returning gifts and taking advantage of the after-Christmas sales.

The first thing Jason found was a new soccer ball for Benny.

Troy's first stop was a stack of boxed chocolates. "Does Salena like chocolate? Wait . . . is chocolate good for the baby?"

"I don't know about the baby, but I don't think Salena needs anything that might cause her to gain more weight."

"Bet you ain't gonna tell her that."

"Uh . . . nope."

"How about this?" Troy held up a red and green knit cap with a pattern of white snowflakes around the rim. "Appropriate, don't you think? And look, it's marked down. Go figure."

"I don't want it to look like I shopped at the clearance table."

"Which you are."

"I don't want it to be obvious."

After searching awhile, Jason found another knit hat with a similar pattern but in blue and white.

"Gloves to match?" Troy held up a pair of blue and white knit gloves.

"Perfect," said Jason. "Now for the baby."

As he perused the jumbles of unclaimed clothing and toys, Jason kept a lookout for anyone who might recognize him. He didn't want to be seen in the children's section at Target.

"Hey, look here," he heard Troy say from the adjoining aisle. When Jason rounded the corner, he found Troy examining another knit cap. It was blue and yellow. "Would this fit a baby?"

Jason had an idea. He walked a few rows down and brought back a baby doll. When he tried the hat on the doll, it fit perfectly. He glanced from side to side and quickly snuck the doll back to the place he'd found it.

"What do babies play with?" Troy asked.

"I'm not sure. Rattles, stuffed animals, stuff like that, I guess."

They found a row with items marked *0-1 year*, where Jason picked up a blue plastic rattle and a small stuffed polar bear. The bear was wearing a Santa hat and a red and green ribbon around its neck. In years to come, it would be proof he had bought his son a gift for his first Christmas. At least Jason would know, even if the baby didn't.

That feeling rose in his chest again, like someone had knocked the breath out of him. He put the thought out of his mind as he moved farther down the aisle and found a small blanket with musical instruments printed on it. He wondered if his son would be a musician. His heart ached as he realized he might never know.

Despite his sadness, Jason was beginning to feel good about his shopping trip when he heard voices approaching. Was one of them Carl Moore's voice? He didn't stick around to find out.

On the way home, Troy asked a question that took Jason totally by surprise. "What you gonna name that baby?"

"That's a song, you know. 'Mary, what you gonna name that baby?'"

"Who but you would know useless musical trivia like that?"

"Actually, I haven't given a thought to the name."

"I bet Salena has. She and her folks will probably want to name him something like José or Alejandro. You know, to reflect his Mexican heritage."

"Actually, they're Cuban. Mr. and Mrs. García came to the U.S. thirty years ago."

"Cuban? How did I not know that?"

"What? You mean I discovered something the all-wise Troy Kirkland didn't know?"

"But now I do, so I'm good. By the way, I distinctly remember your man Carl making remarks about Salena being Mexican. You didn't correct him."

"First off, Carl's not my man. Second, why waste my time? Carl probably doesn't even know the difference."

"Thanks for assuming I do."

"You do, don't you?"

"Sure. Cuba's the capital of Puerto Rico, right?"

* * * * *

JASON'S MOTHER was predictable. When he showed her the things he'd bought, she smiled and then burst into tears. She flung her arms around her son and then hurried out of the room. He wondered if he should follow her to see if she was okay, but then he thought better of it. Mom was just being Mom.

He found a couple of empty boxes and some leftover Christmas paper and did his best to wrap the things he had bought Salena and the baby. He just stuck a big red bow on the soccer ball.

The easy part was done. Now he had to somehow get close enough to Salena to give her the gifts. When he dialed her number, he got no answer. After trying three more times, he decided to try the Garcías' land line. Salena's grandmother told him Salena wasn't available.

The same thing happened the next day and then the next. He was beginning to get the picture. Finally, he explained to Mrs. García why he was trying to contact Salena and asked if he could come by and drop off the gifts. She said okay, and he offered to come by tomorrow, which was New Year's Day.

* * * * *

Wednesday, January 1

WHEN HE rang the doorbell, Mrs. García answered quickly. Jason heard a noise somewhere in the house. "Is Salena here?"

"Yes, but she is busy now." Mrs. García reached for the gifts. "Thank you, Jason. I will give these to Salena."

"The ball is for Benny."

"Oh, yes. *Gracias.*"

As he was leaving, he heard Benny's voice from down the hallway. "Mommi, can I come out and see Jason?"

Jason hadn't noticed the truck in the driveway, so he was surprised to hear Mr. García's voice. "No, you must not see him again."

"It's not fair!" Benny whined. "Even if Jason's not Salena's boyfriend he's still my friend."

Mrs. García gave Jason an uneasy look and began to shut the door. There was the sound of a scuffle down the hallway, ending with the slamming of a door.

"No, Benito," Jason heard Mr. García say. "You will not leave this room."

Benny began screeching like a wounded animal.

Jason stepped back inside. "May I talk to him? Maybe I can calm him down."

Mrs. García disappeared down the hallway for a minute and then returned. She swung the door open wider, which Jason took as a signal to come in.

In Benny's room, Jason found Mr. García standing beside the bed with his arms folded and a scowl on his face. Benny sat on the opposite side of the bed, his face red and tears streaming down his cheeks.

"Jason!" Benny shouted. "Where have you been? Don't you like me anymore?"

Jason glanced at Mr. García, and he joined his wife in the doorway. Benny stood with his fist out. Jason stepped up so they could exchange their special fist-bump greeting.

"Sure I do, B. Just because I don't come around doesn't mean I don't like you."

"It's Salena's fault, isn't it?"

"No, B, it's my fault."

"How come?"

Jason glanced at Mr. and Mrs. García. "Someday you'll understand. For now, just trust me, okay?"

Benny looked like he was about to cry again.

"Okay?" Jason repeated.

"Okay. But you can still come and see *me*."

Jason looked at the grandparents and Mrs. García looked at her husband.

"If it means so much to Benito," said Mr. García. "But it's Salena's choice whether she wants to see you."

"I understand. How is Salena, by the way?"

"As good as can be expected," said Mrs. García.

It wasn't much information.

Jason exchanged another fist-bump with Benny, said goodbye, and left.

*****

Monday, January 6

SCHOOL RESUMED on Monday. It was the beginning of a new semester, so some of Jason's classes were different. He kept his eyes peeled for Salena but assumed she was still avoiding him on purpose. Later that week, he learned something that made him wish that's all it was.

CHAPTER 16

Friday, January 10

AFTER LEAVING D.B. in the parking lot, Jason hoisted his heavy bag onto his shoulder and headed toward the gym to find Troy and claim their usual perch at the top of the bleachers to wait for the first bell. Before he got to the gym, one of Salena's bodyguards stopped him. He assumed she intended to hurl one of her usual barbs, but she didn't.

"Hey, Jason, did you hear what happened?"

His first thought was that Salena had been in an accident. His second thought was that she had gone into labor. Was he already a father? Shouldn't someone have told him? And wasn't it way too early for the baby to be born? "I haven't heard anything. I haven't seen Salena at school. Did something happen to her?"

"Her grandfather had an accident."

"Oh, no! How bad is he hurt?"

"I'm not sure, but I hear he's still in the hospital."

"That's terrible! Thanks for telling me. I'll try to check on him."

As the day crept by, Jason could hardly concentrate on school. That afternoon, he called Cal to let him know he would be running late. Cal said he understood but try not to make it too long.

When he got to the hospital, he found Ms. García in the Intensive Care waiting room. She explained that Sergio had fallen off a ladder at work on Monday. He not only shattered his right hip but sustained a compound fracture of both bones below his right elbow, requiring complicated surgery.

"How are Salena and Benny taking it?"

"Salena is okay. She is staying at home with Benny. Benny is convinced his *abuelo* is dying."

"He's not, is he?"

"No, praise God. He is improving so far, but it is questionable whether he will ever walk again."

"You mind if I go see Benny?"

Mrs. García shook her head. "I appreciate it. Maybe you can reassure him."

Jason left the hospital and sped across town to the Garcías' house. Salena answered the door and actually seemed happy to see him as she stepped aside so he could come in.

"I heard what happened. I've been wondering why you weren't at school. I was afraid—" he pointed toward Salena's ever-expanding midsection "—you know."

"Thanks, but no, we're fine."

"You're pretty as ever."

"*¡Mentiroso!*"

"I'm not lying."

"Yeah, whatever." Salena gave a dismissive wave of her hand.

"Anyway, I just talked to your *abuela* at the hospital. In case you're wondering, I came to see Benny."

He found Benny sitting on the living room floor, leaning against the couch. Some game show was on TV, but he didn't seem to be paying attention to it. Salena grabbed the remote and hit the OFF button.

Jason dropped to the floor beside Benny. "Hey, B."

Benny stared at the floor. "Did you know Poppi's going to die?"

"No he's not. I just came from the hospital. Mommi told me Poppi's a little better now."

Benny's head jerked up. "For real?"

Jason nodded. "For real."

"We've been telling him that," said Salena. "He doesn't believe us."

"When is he coming home?" Benny asked.

"I'm sure it'll be a few more days. He broke his hip, you know, and his arm's hurt pretty bad, too."

"Will you come back again?"

"Sure, if your family doesn't mind." He looked over at Salena.

"It's okay."

Before he got up and headed for the door, Jason exchanged a fist-bump with Benny. "You got a joke for me?"

"Not today. I don't feel like it."

"I understand. Check you later, all right?"

"Okay, Jason."

"I'm glad you dropped by," said Salena. "To see Benny."

"No problem. When you coming back to school?"

"I'm not sure. Mommi wants to keep Benny home for a few days, and someone has to stay with him while she's stuck at the hospital."

"See you later?"

Salena just wiggled her head and shrugged, as if to say *whatever*. It wasn't the response Jason had hoped for.

CHAPTER 17

Monday, January 13

JASON WAS glad to see Salena back at school on Monday. When he caught up with her in the cafeteria and inquired about her grandfather, she said Poppi was out of ICU. Benny had gone for a visit and seemed reassured. He also was happy to be back in school.

Jason made a point to drop by the hospital before work that evening. He was surprised to see Sergio sitting in the bedside chair trying to eat dinner with his left hand. His right arm was wrapped in a big bandage. His wife sat at his side.

"*Buenas Noches, Señor García. ¿Como está usted?*"

"*Muy bién,*" Mr. García answered, meaning he was very well.

"I'm glad to see you're better."

"Oh, no need to worry about me. I am, how you say, strong as the ox."

Jason sat on the side of the bed, putting himself closer to Mr. García's eye level. "It looks like you have a pretty good thing going here."

Mr. García bobbed his head toward his wife. "Ari thinks I am helpless. She treats me like a *niño*."

"I wouldn't have to treat you like a child if you would take better care of yourself." Mrs. García's voice was stern. "You gave me a terrible scare, you know."

Mr. García's face softened a little. "Yes, I know, *mi amor*. But I am fine. Stop worrying!"

Over her husband's head, Mrs. García caught Jason's eye. She wore a pained expression, with her eyebrows pinched together.

Mr. García's fork slipped out of his hand and clattered to the floor, splattering mashed potatoes everywhere. "I am wasting time in this hospital," he grumbled. "I need to be at work."

Mrs. García flashed another concerned look in Jason's direction. "He can't go home until he begins *rehabilitación*."

"I'll be rooting for you," said Jason.

Mr. García looked confused. "What is this rooting?"

"Pulling for you. Cheering you on."

"And praying?" asked Mrs. García.

"Oh, sure. And praying." Jason glanced at the time on his phone. "I need to get something to eat before I go to work."

Mrs. García stood up. "I'll walk out with you." As soon as they were out of earshot, she placed a hand on Jason's arm. He could see the concern in her eyes. "Jason, I have to tell somebody. I don't tell Salena and Benny. Especially Benny."

"Is *Señor* García okay?"

"Not as good as he thinks. The doctor told us today Sergio might not be able to go back to work."

"He doesn't seem worried."

"He thinks he is hiding it from me. It is hard for him to accept."

"Won't rehab help?"

"His injuries are very severe. At his age, the hip will take a long time to heal, if it heals at all. And how is he going to do any work with his left hand? You saw what a mess he is making of his dinner. If he doesn't go back to work, what will he do with himself? He has worked so hard all his life. Thank God the accident didn't kill him, but not being able to work might. And now—" She looked away, as if trying to decide whether to go on.

Jason suspected what was on her mind. "And now you will have another mouth to feed, not to mention the other expenses the baby will bring."

Mrs. García's eyes began to fill with tears.

"*Señora* García, I'm sorry."

Mrs. García wiped her face with the back of her hand and silently turned toward her husband's hospital room.

* * * * *

THE REST of the week was a blur. Jason forced himself to keep up the routine of school, work, visiting the hospital when he could, and working with the weights at home. Every night, he fell into bed exhausted. But that didn't mean he slept. Sleep was getting harder to come by.

* * * * *

Monday, January 20

SCHOOL WAS out for Martin Luther King Day. For some reason—perhaps the alignment of the stars or maybe the world had completely stopped turning—Jason didn't have to work. This was a good thing because last night had been another without much sleep. During bouts of wakefulness, his thoughts continually churned. But, unlike all the other sleepless nights, this one wasn't totally wasted, for he'd come up with another plan.

CHAPTER 18

Friday, January 24

As USUAL, Salena managed to avoid him all week. Nor would she answer his phone calls. He finally resorted to texting her to say he needed to talk to her. He didn't want to tell her much in a text. This was too important to say in a text.

To his surprise, she looked him up at school on Friday. He tried not to sound desperate when he asked if he could come to her house on Saturday. He said it would not only give him a chance to connect with Benny but would also allow him to see how her grandfather was getting along.

"He didn't come home," she told him. "He's gone to a rehab hospital."

"How long?"

"Depends on how well he does." Salena's dark eyebrows clenched together. "Since when did you start biting your fingernails?"

Jason hadn't even been aware he was doing that. When he examined his left hand, he discovered that all the nails were chewed down to nubs. He shoved both hands into his pockets. "So how is he doing? Your *abuelo*."

"Not very well. It's slow. He thinks he should be back at a hundred percent already. But he might never be."

"So can I come tomorrow anyway? I need to talk to you about some stuff."

She told him to come around eleven.

* * * * *

Saturday, January 25

HE PULLED up at Salena's house precisely at eleven. Benny came to the door, and the two of them exchanged their usual greeting. Mommi was gone to visit Poppi.

Jason hoped Salena would tell Benny to go to his room. When she didn't, Jason asked him to do it. Benny agreed, on the condition that Jason would talk to him again before he left.

Jason and Salena sat on the couch, facing each other but not touching. There seemed to be no good place to begin.

"Salena, please don't say anything until you hear me out. Okay?"

She tilted her head and frowned. "I guess so. What is it?"

"Look, I've told you a hundred times how sorry I am to have put you and your family in this situation. But there's nothing we can do about it now. And if Poppi can't go back to work, it will put a financial strain on all of you."

"You think we're destitute?"

"No, I didn't mean that. But it will have to be more difficult now."

"I gather you have some big problem-solving plan."

"Marry me, Salena." Jason waited for Salena's reaction. She just stared at him. "Say something."

"Why does this sound familiar?"

"I know. I messed it all up the other time. This time, I've given it a lot of thought. I really think we should get married. It will be easier on your grandparents, and by the time the baby comes, we should have our own place."

Salena smiled. "Jason, you dope. You poor, sweet dope."

"What? Why?"

"You think I'll be better off with you than with Poppi and Mommi? How can you support a family on what you make at Cal's?"

"I'll get a better job."

"What kind of job is going to pay enough? You're still seventeen."

"I'll be eighteen this year. So will you."

"We're no different than when we went through this two months ago. Just because you're eighteen won't mean you'll be ready for a fulltime job. And we still don't know anything about making it on our own or taking care of a baby."

"We'll learn. Everyone has to start somewhere. We can make it work. I know we can."

"What about college?"

"I'm staying here, remember? When we get everything straightened out, I can enroll at Arkansas State. It'll be okay for now. When I'm not relying on my parents, I should qualify for grants or something. I'm sure Ms. Carter can help me with that."

"Does ASU have the kind of music program you want?"

"I don't care about that anymore. I'll choose something more practical. If nothing else, it'll make my dad happy. And Mom will be glad if I stay closer to home. That's worth something."

"But *you* will be miserable."

"So will you. We'll be miserable together." He smiled, which prompted Salena to smile also. "I can't think of anyone I'd rather be miserable with."

The smile quickly left Salena's face. "Jason—" she briefly turned away, as if searching for the right words "—I have to tell you something."

"Sure. Anything."

"The truth is, I don't love you. I thought I did, and I think you thought you loved me. But just because we made a baby doesn't mean we really care for each other. What kind of life will that be? Especially for the baby."

"In time, we'll grow to love one another."

"There's no guarantee. What if we grow to hate one another instead?"

He couldn't answer for a moment. Then, forbidding himself to cry, he raised his right hand. "Salena Marisol García, I solemnly promise to never hate you."

Salena jumped and then took Jason's hand and placed it on her round stomach. "Feel that."

When he felt the baby give a strong kick, Jason could no longer hold back the flood of tears. "That's amazing! It's like he's saying he approves."

Salena smiled. "Well, he's not the boss yet."

Jason shook his head with mock seriousness. "Of course not. We're the parents, not him. Oh, my goodness, I sound just like my dad."

"Someday you'll make a good dad."

Jason smeared the tears from his face with the back of his hand. "Promise me you'll think it over."

"Give me a week."

"A week?"

"This isn't something we should decide on a whim."

"You're right. Fair enough. Next Saturday, same time, same, er, station?"

"Yeah, I guess."

"You gonna tell your *abuelos*?"

Before Salena could reply, a voice shouted from down the hallway. "Yippee! Jason and Salena are getting married!"

"I'm guessing it won't be a secret long," said Salena.

CHAPTER 19

ANOTHER WAITING game. At least it wouldn't be so long this time. There were moments during the week when Jason was certain he had done the right thing to ask Salena—again—to marry him. Other times—most of the time—it scared him more than he wanted to admit.

Married at 17? He knew Dee Watson was right when he said the odds were stacked against them. And Salena was right, too. Just because she and Jason had a baby didn't mean they were capable of being proper parents. But maybe all first-time parents felt this way, regardless of their age. He'd heard it said that babies don't come with an owner's manual. Yet the majority of children grow up to be functional adults.

He thought about Benny. What would it be like to raise a child with special needs? But Benny's disability wasn't genetic. It presumably had something to do with their mother falling in with the wrong crowd when she was pregnant the second time. No telling what Benny endured before he was born.

Jason didn't know much about Salena and Benny's father. All he knew was that when Benito Sr. found out his son wasn't normal, he left. Until a couple of months ago, Salena didn't even know where her father was.

But none of this had anything to do with Jason and Salena. Salena was not like her mother. And Jason was certainly not like her father.

* * * * *

Wednesday, January 29

JASON HAPPENED to see Ms. Carter in the hall and arranged to speak with her after school. She showed him where to find grant applications online and explained what information he would need to provide. Of course, he would have to get his parents involved, which Jason hoped wouldn't be a problem. It all sounded fairly simple, except for one thing. Some of the deadlines for applying had passed and others were swiftly approaching. Ms. Carter promised to expedite the process as much as she could.

On a whim, he decided to make some calls to find out how much an apartment would cost. He later regretted he'd done it, as what he learned frightened him even more. He'd had no idea how much rent would be. Worse, the first payment would have to cover the first month's rent plus a "maintenance deposit"—whatever that meant—of two or three hundred dollars. How would he come up with that kind of money all at the same time?

At one point, he wondered how to apply for government housing. He quickly put this out of his mind. He would not become one of those people. He would do whatever it took to make sure he and Salena could make it on their own.

* * * * *

Saturday, February 1

As USUAL, Jason hardly got a glimpse of Salena all week. But they had a deal. He texted her early Saturday morning and said he was on his way.

Benny met him at the door and then disappeared into the living room, where the TV was playing. Mrs. García said she wouldn't be going to visit Sergio until later in the day. She wanted to be present when Jason and Salena spoke. She invited Jason into the kitchen and offered him a glass of tea or a soda. He declined, but they sat at the kitchen table anyway. He knew Salena knew why he was there, so he let her talk first.

She glanced at Mommi and then looked him squarely in the eye. "Jason, I'm sorry if you're hurt, but I'm not going to marry you."

Jason looked from Salena to her grandmother.

"Sergio and I still believe a child should have two parents and they should be married. But now it is our own family, we are not sure what is best. We must leave it up to our granddaughter. It is her life."

"I had a little help," Salena said. "Mommi and I talked to Sister Margaret at the church."

"She was a great help," said Mrs. García. "In spite of her age, Sister Margaret knows times have changed, and she understands how it is between boys and girls these days. We have confidence in her faith and very much appreciate her opinion."

"She helped me to see it would be unwise for us to get married."

"But what about the baby?"

"Sister Margaret suggested I reconsider putting the baby up for adoption."

"So? Is that what you're going to do?" Jason looked from Salena to Mrs. García.

"It still does not seem right," said Mrs. García. "This is our flesh and blood. But Sergio and I will support Salena's decision."

Salena reached into the pocket of her baggie hoodie and handed Jason a tiny velvet box. When he opened it, he found the promise ring he had given her two Christmases ago.

"I want you to keep the ring," he said. "As a memento of promises made, even if they weren't kept."

"That's not necessary."

"Please." He handed the box back to her. "I want you to have it."

Salena snapped the box shut and held it in both hands. "It will always be special to me."

Jason glanced at the clock above the cook stove. He still had a couple of hours before work, but there was nothing else to say to Salena or her grandmother.

CHAPTER 20

"Now, LET me see . . ." Troy made a show of scratching his head. "Is this Plan B or Plan C?"

"More like F or G," said Jason as they pulled up in front of Troy's house.

Troy checked the clock on the dashboard before getting out. "How much time you got?"

"Actually, I don't have to work tonight. I think I'll just go home and crash."

"After you finish your trig homework, of course."

Jason made a gagging noise. "You had to remind me."

"So this new plan—F, or G, or whatever it is—how is it supposed to work? I thought you said Salena's giving the baby up for adoption."

"That's what she and her grandparents want to do. It doesn't seem right. I want to be there for my son."

"Very noble of you, my friend. You gonna ask your dad for help?"

"Are you kidding? And give him the satisfaction of knowing I'm a total failure?"

"Then what *are* you gonna do?"

"Lucky for me, Cal's night manager's leaving the first of March. Cal's going to let me try the manager position. If I work every evening through the week and every other weekend, I should be able to afford my own place eventually."

"And say good-bye to life as you know it."

"Desperate times . . . ." Jason bit the nail off his right index finger and swiped his hand on his pants.

"And what's Junior gonna be doing while you're working your life away?"

"I'm hoping to sweet talk Mom into helping with the baby. That is, unless Dad flips out—which he probably will."

"And what if it doesn't work out? Pretty sure a baby's not something you can just toss aside."

"I'll drop out of school and get a fulltime job."

"Oh, man! Your dad's gonna love that."

"At least I won't be under his thumb anymore. Or his precious roof."

"And here's a happy thought. No girl's gonna want to date a guy who already has a kid. You know that, don't you?"

Jason started to bite another fingernail but crossed his arms instead. "I think I'm done with women anyway."

"Dude, you are one pitiful puppy!"

Jason gave a silent shrug.

"And college?"

Jason shrugged again.

"Well, you know *I'm* always here for you."

Jason smirked. "For loans? Babysitting?"

Troy gave his glasses a nervous nudge. "You know I don't have any money. And Uncle Troy don't know nothing about babies."

"So you're here for me how?"

Troy looked down and turned to get out of the car.

"I'm sorry," Jason said. "Truth is, you've always been here for me. You really are a good friend, you know that?"

Troy turned back and smiled widely. "Now that's more like it."

"You're still not gonna hug me."

"Yeah, I know."

CHAPTER 21

THE PAST couple of years, Jason had welcomed every opportunity to do something special for Salena. A movie, a meal—the best he could afford, which was never very much—or a card. She wasn't hard to please.

This year was different. Valentine's Day had gone the way of all the other holidays. He doubted Salena expected, or even wanted, anything from him. But she was the mother of his child. How could he pretend she meant nothing to him?

On the way to school, he swung by Walmart, where he'd seen colorful bouquets wrapped in cellophane. He chose one with yellow and white daisies. Glancing at his phone, he confirmed that he had time to stop on the greeting card aisle. He found a card that said, "To a special someone on Valentine's Day." It was noncommittal enough. Before he left the parking lot, he opened the card and jotted "Love, Jason" as he'd always done. He wasn't sure she would appreciate it, but he wouldn't let that bother him.

When he got to school, he waited on the steps outside the gym until Salena arrived. As soon as she saw him, her eyes popped open, and then she managed a faint smile. He handed her the flowers and the card and walked away. Neither of them spoke.

* * * * *

Saturday, February 22

JASON WAS startled when his phone rang on the way to work. He had a little extra time, so he pulled into a parking lot and stopped. For a split second, he wondered if it was Salena. Of course, it wasn't. He couldn't believe whose voice he heard.

"Hey, bro!"

"Derek?"

"Thought I'd check up on my little brother and see if he's staying out of trouble."

"Haven't you heard?"

"Oh, I've heard. Mom told me everything a while back."

"Figures."

"Sounds like you've got yourself into kind of a mess."

"You think?"

"When's the kid due?"

"Mid-April."

"Yikes! That's close. What you gonna do?"

Jason heaved a sigh. "I don't want to tell you. I'm afraid it'll fall through, like everything else I've come up with."

"Yeah, I know what you mean."

"Oh, come on! Things always go your way."

"I'm sorry. I thought you knew who you were talking to. This is your brother. Remember me?"

"What you talking about?"

"In what universe do you think things always go *anybody's* way? Especially mine."

"That's how it looked to me."

"Really?"

"Uh . . . yeah. Do you have any idea how hard it is to be Derek Sadler's kid brother?"

"How come?"

"For starters, you're everyone's favorite, including Mom and Dad. Even Troy idolizes you."

"Is that guy gay?"

"Nah, just weird."

"Well, so maybe I've caught a few breaks," Derek continued, "but I've had my share of problems, too. Take it from me, life ain't easy at the top."

"Could have fooled me."

"I was never aware you were interested in my life."

"I always looked up to you, even though you ignored me."

"Okay, true, we *have* been sort of out of touch the last few years."

"From where I stood, you always seemed to have it made in the shade."

Derek's heavy sigh was obvious over the phone, followed by silence.

"Okay, Derek, when you gonna tell me the real reason you called?"

"The fact is, I need to run something by you. I'm trying to work up the nerve to tell Mom and Dad I'm making a career out of the Army."

"You serious? What brought this on all of a sudden?"

"Actually, I've been thinking about it for a while."

"You mean no Don & Derek Sadler, CPA's?"

"Where'd you get that idea?"

"I just thought—you know, you and Dad."

"Dad and I don't get along. You think I could work with him?"

"Okay, now I *don't* know who I'm talking to."

"Jason, I only managed to stay on Dad's good side because I went along with everything he said. I hated it. Why do you think I joined the Army as soon as I could?"

"Because that's what you do. Always the hometown hero."

"Do I detect some sarcasm in that whiny voice of yours?" A hint of humor softened Derek's words.

"That's an understatement. The sarcasm, that is."

"Look, little bro, I'm almost out of time."

"Me too."

"Oh wait, I need to tell you something else. I got my next assignment."

"Afghanistan?"

"Unfortunately. I'm heading to Fort Riley, Kansas, in a couple of weeks to begin training with The Big Red One."

"The what?"

"For you unenlightened folk, that's the 1st Infantry Division."

"Mom's gonna freak out."

Derek blew out a loud breath. "Yeah, I know."

Jason glanced at the clock on the dashboard. "Hey, I have five minutes to get to Cal's. I'm really glad you called, Derek. Let's talk again sometime."

"Yeah, we will. Tell Mom I'll call soon. But don't tell her why, okay?"

"Don't worry. I think I've been the source of enough bad news lately. But one good thing—maybe this will take Mom and Dad's attention off me for a while."

"Uh, you're welcome. Anyway, take care, okay?"

Jason punched his phone off and pulled onto the street. As he drove, the thought occurred to him that he could also join the Army. It would be a steady paycheck. But no, that would defeat his whole purpose, which was to provide a home for his son.

He thought back to the day he had called to find information about apartment rental. Would the new job provide enough money for rent, the security deposit, food, clothing, supplies for the baby? The baby? He had no idea what he would need for the baby. Hopefully his mother would help him with that. He doubted Salena would be any help. She had made it clear she didn't want to be saddled with the responsibilities of motherhood.

Derek was right. Mid-April loomed awfully close. Was two months enough time to figure it all out?

* * * * *

Sunday, March 8

"So, how's the new job going?" Troy popped his laptop open on Jason's bed.

"Okay so far." Jason stared at the blank screen on which he was supposed to be writing an essay for English tomorrow. "It's a lot more responsibility, but Cal's letting me start slow."

"Big bucks now, huh?"

"Not exactly. At least I don't have to rely on tips anymore. Gotta say, all those schmoozing skills I learned come in handy now that I'm a manager."

"Any luck finding a place for you and Junior to live?"

"I haven't told you about that?"

"Nope."

"Dee Watson put me in touch with a guy who has a cheap apartment over his garage. Emphasis on *cheap*."

"What's it look like?"

"It's not much. Reckon I don't need much anyway. Rent's not as bad as I thought it would be. The guy felt sorry for me, so he's not charging me a security deposit, long as I don't wreck anything."

"What about all those wild parties we're gonna have?"

Jason smirked. "Uh-huh."

"How's your mom and dad handling it?"

"The usual. Mom cried. Dad hasn't said much. His main concern is how I'll keep up with my school work."

"Which brings us back to . . ." Troy bobbed his head toward the blank screens they both held in their laps.

Jason spit out a splinter of fingernail. "What you writing about?"

"I'm gonna write about how cool it would be at the ripe old age of seventeen to be living on my own."

"Want to trade places with me?"

"You kiddin'? Not for love nor monkeys I'm trading places with you."

"That's what I thought."

"Dude, are sucking your thumb?"

Jason spit out a strip of skin he had bitten off. "Shut up, Troy."

CHAPTER 22

JASON'S STOMACH clenched as he sped across town. "Of course this would happen," he muttered as he blew a blood-tinged sliver of fingernail out the window. "Nothing goes the way I plan."

It was the day he had looked forward to. And dreaded. He wasn't ready. The truth was, he wouldn't have been ready even if hadn't happened a month early.

He had spoken to the band and choir directors a couple of weeks ago to explain that he might miss some afterschool practices, concerts, and games. Because it would be so late in the school year, they agreed to give Jason time to try it out before it became necessary to drop the classes altogether. Now, with a dull pang of regret, Jason accepted that he would need to go ahead and give it all up.

His mother hadn't appeared unhappy at the prospect of taking care of her first grandchild. She had already put in notice that she would resign her job when the baby came. So far, his father hadn't expressed any objection.

* * * * *

THE NEAREST available parking space was far from the entrance of the hospital. Marching band practice and four months of workouts with his brother's weights had built up his stamina so he had no problem sprinting to the building. He forced himself to slow down as the automatic door slid open.

After a quick scan of the hospital directory beside the elevator, he stepped inside and punched the button for the third floor. When he stepped out of the elevator, he was greeted by Mrs. García.

"Any news yet?" he asked.

"Not for a while. Last we heard, everything is going as expected."

Benny and his grandfather were sitting off to one side, doing their best to avoid other people. Mr. García was in a wheelchair.

"Hey, Jason," Benny said. "Did you know I'm going to be *un tio?*"

"An uncle. Yeah, that's the way it works."

"And you'll be *un padre.*"

Jason nodded. "Looks that way."

"How can you be a father when you're so young?"

"I've asked myself that question a bunch of times." He turned back to Mrs. García and lowered his voice. "Is *Señor* García confined to a wheelchair now?"

"Yes, and he hates it. He has lost confidence in the *rehabilitación*. He is very impatient."

Just then, Jason's mother stepped out of the elevator. "I came as soon as I heard. Don will come if he can get away." She hugged Mrs. García and then Jason.

"No word yet," said Jason.

After a minute of awkward silence, Mrs. García surprised them with more news. "Guess what. I'm going to work."

"Really?" Jason asked.

"I thought about it a lot since the visit with Sister Margaret. I am starting to believe God doesn't expect every woman to sit at home and depend on a man to support her."

"Well," said Mrs. Sadler, "I certainly believe it's a woman's prerogative if she wants to work."

Jason glanced across the room. "Does Poppi agree?"

"Of course not," said Mrs García. "He's so old-fashioned and set in his ways. It's one of the things I love about him. But things are different now."

"Have you begun looking yet?" asked Mrs. Sadler.

"Oh, yes, I already have a job. I will be working in the school cafeteria."

"Will you be cooking for us at the high school?" asked Jason.

"No, I will be at the middle school."

Jason smiled. "Well, considering your skill at cooking, I'd say you'll fit right in."

"This is my hope. I know I have a lot to learn. I have never worked outside the home before."

Jason glanced over to make sure Mr. García couldn't hear the conversation. "Is he going to be able to go back to work? If he stops rehab, his recovery will stop too, won't it?"

"Try telling him that."

And then Jason had an idea. He went over and sat next to Mr. García. "*Señor* García, I'm going to join a gym. Why don't you try it with me?"

Mr. García looked puzzled.

"A gym," Jason repeated. "*Un gimnasio.*"

"*¿Un gimnasio?* How do I have time to go to *un gimnasio?*"

"Looks to me like you got all the time in the world. I hear you're unhappy with your rehab. Maybe you could work on your hip and your arm while I continue my weight lifting."

"Can I join too?" asked Benny.

"We cannot go to *un gimnasio*. We cannot afford such a thing."

"Actually, I know of one that is offering the first month free for new members. There's no obligation to continue. Why don't you and Benny try it? After that, you can decide whether to stick with it."

Jason noticed his mother and Mrs. García were listening to the conversation.

"I never heard of such a thing," said Mrs. García. "Is it even possible?"

"It's worth a try," said Mrs. Sadler. "I know some physical therapists. I'll see if they can work out an agreement with your doctors and the gym."

"*Anything* would be better than nothing," said Jason.

"Sergio, listen to these people," said Mrs. García. "They are trying to help you finish your *rehabilitación*. It is the only hope you have for returning to work." From the look on Mrs. García's face, Jason got the feeling her husband would be joining the gym whether he liked it or not.

"If we join at the same time, we can be each other's workout partner," Jason added.

"Me, too?"

"Sure, B, if it's okay with Poppi."

Mr. García almost smiled. "We will, how you say, *root* for one another?"

"That's the idea."

Just then the doctor appeared. "Mr. and Mrs. García, you have a new grandson."

"Actually, it is our great-grandson," said Mrs. García. "Salena is our granddaughter."

"I see." He looked at Jason. "Are you the father?"

"Yes, sir."

"Then I guess congratulations are in order." He shook Jason's hand.

"Thank you. Is Salena okay?"

"Oh, yes, she's fine."

"And the baby?"

"A big, healthy boy. I understand he will be put up for adoption."

"This is what we think is best," said Sergio.

"Then I will arrange for a social worker to come and talk to all of you."

Jason thought about telling them his plan but decided to wait, in case he changed his mind.

"Can we see the baby?" asked Benny.

"It's up to your family. In adoption cases, I don't usually recommend it."

"When can we see Salena?" Jason asked.

"Whenever she feels like it. The nurse will let you know."

* * * * *

AFTER ABOUT an hour, a nurse came and led the family to Salena's room. She was asleep but woke up when they went in. She looked tired, and her hair was messed up. Mommi and Benny took turns hugging her. Jason just leaned in and kissed her on the forehead. Jason's mother also gave Salena a quick hug. By that time, Mr. Garcia had rolled close to the bed. With much effort, he pulled himself up and hugged Salena with his left arm and then dropped back into the wheelchair, wincing from pain.

Mrs. García took a brush from her purse and began to smooth Salena's hair.

"Leave her alone, Ari," Sergio said, still breathing heavily. "She's beautiful already."

"Poppi, you know you are not a good liar."

Sergio gave Salena a faint smile. "You will always be beautiful to me."

"Am I an uncle?" Benny asked. "I don't feel any different."

Salena smiled. "How did you expect to feel?"

"I don't know. I've never been an uncle before." He turned to Jason. "How does it feel to be a father?"

"I'm not sure. It's new to me, too."

"Well," said Mrs. Sadler, "I, for one, feel awfully old now that I'm a grandmother."

Mrs. García smiled. "You are a very young grandmother. But you will get used to it." She gazed from Salena to Jason and then spoke to Sergio and Benny. "Why don't we go look for something to eat? You hungry, Benito?"

"I'm starving!"

"Why do I bother to ask?" She turned to Mrs. Sadler. "You are welcome to join us."

"Thanks, but I need to go back to work."

After they were gone, Jason stood beside Salena's bed and took her hand. "You feel okay?"

"Um, I guess so. I just had a baby, you know."

"So I hear."

Salena's eyes searched Jason's. "Have you seen him?"

"Not yet. Did *you* see him? I mean . . . you *were* in the room when he was born."

Salena shook her head. "I just heard him crying. I wanted to see him." Tears began to flow down her cheek. "I wanted to hold my baby."

Jason brushed Salena's hair away from her face. "I know."

"Jason, you have to go see him. I want to know what he looks like. And I have to know he's okay."

"He's okay. They already told me."

"No, I mean okay about not knowing his mother and father."

"He was just born. He doesn't know about that."

"Jason, listen to me. You have to see him so you can tell me about him."

"Let's go together."

Salena's tears began to flow profusely. "No. I'm afraid I won't be able to stand it. I'm afraid I won't be able to let him go."

"You don't have to do that. We can keep him."

Salena managed a smile in spite of her tears. "He's not a puppy, you know."

"I didn't mean it to sound that way."

"You're still willing to get married?"

"Of course I am."

Salena and Jason held hands while Salena sobbed, and then she looked into Jason's eyes. "I haven't changed my mind. I still don't want to get married. And how can I force a baby on Mommi and Poppi?"

Jason was silent as tears began to stream down his own face. "Then *I'll* do it myself."

"Do what?"

"I'm going to raise our baby, with or without you."

"How can you possibly do that?"

"It'll be a challenge I know, but that doesn't mean I can't do it."

"Your parents are okay with you bringing the baby to your house?"

"It's not up to them. I have my own place. I've already paid a hundred dollars to hold it till the first of April."

"And you're sure you want to do this?"

"In a way, no. In another, I've never been so sure of anything."

Jason handed Salena a tissue from the box by the bed and then swiped his own face with the back of his hand. He lifted Salena's hand and kissed it. "See you later," he said as he turned and left the room.

Just outside the door was a sign with an arrow pointing the way to the nursery. He began walking resolutely but slowed as he neared the last corner.

Somewhere a baby was crying. He wondered if it was his, but he was afraid to find out. What if he saw his newborn son in distress and panicked? Would he turn tail and run away?

How could he raise a child by himself? The baby didn't even have a name. Was Salena right? Was this a ridiculous idea?

As he rounded the corner, he stopped. He couldn't believe what he saw.

* * * * *

"MOM! DAD! What are you doing here?"

"Oh, Jason!" said his mother. "I couldn't leave without seeing my grandbaby. He's beautiful!"

"Mom, I—"

"Come on, Son," said Dad. "You need to see him. He's the spitting image of you."

"Dad, I'm afraid. What if . . . ."

Mom stepped across the corridor and hugged her seventeen-year-old son who had just become a father. She stepped back at arm's length and looked him in the eyes. "Jason, your father and I have something to tell you."

Jason's eyes bounced between his mother and father.

"We've made a decision," his mother continued. "We don't want you to do this by yourself. We want you and the baby to stay with us."

Jason looked at his father. "Really?"

"Really," said Dad. "We'll even look into adopting him. That is, if it's okay with you."

"This isn't something you should decide in a hurry."

"We agree," said Mom. "And we haven't. Actually, we've been talking about it for a couple of weeks. We didn't want to say anything until we found out if it could work."

"Do Salena's folks know?"

Dad nodded. "We spoke with them a couple of days ago. They seem to be warming up to the idea. We thought we had more time to prepare and to discuss it with you and Salena, but the baby surprised us."

"We all live close enough to work together," said Mom. "Arianny and I will devise a schedule. I'm quitting my job anyway, and hers will only be half-days and during the school year.

"Does this mean I can go to college?"

"The six of us need to talk about that," said Dad. "Of course, your mother and I want you to go to college. Salena, too, if possible. But we want you to stay local. We expect the two of you to pull your share of the load."

"Fair enough."

"And now," said Dad, as he swept his hand toward the nursery window, "I think it's time to go say hello to your new son.

A retired school counselor and Licensed Professional Counselor, Sam L. Sullivan lives on a farm in northeast Arkansas. He is an Army veteran and spent 11 months in Vietnam in the early 70's. He and his wife Jan raised two sons and have one grandson.

Previous works include "Deep Well, Sweet Water" (2017), "Ring Around Rose" (2018), "The Ghost of Weasel's Valley" (2018), and "The Best Spelr in the Kingdum (Werld) (2019). In the 70's, Sullivan wrote the song "There Never Was A Pulpit Like the Cross," which was recorded by an acappella group and can be heard on YouTube.